OLOF:

THE

IMPRISONED

By Trinth Dupree (U.Donn)

ISBN 978-0-6152-4333-7

Text copyright 2008 by Trinth Dupree

All rights reserved. Published by U. Donn

Acknowledgements

I would like to thank my Lord and Savior Jesus Christ who spared me and saved me from my destructive ways. My dear wife, Andrea who has inspired me and been by my side the entire way. Thank you for putting up with me these fourteen years of our eternal marriage. Nisha, my oldest daughter that looks just like me and has a writing talent that exceeds her age, keep it up it is going to pay off. Marie, my youngest daughter, who hates to write but has tremendous talent. She is the artist who will make us rich someday. TJ, my son, the worshipper of the crew will never stop singing and we love to hear that voice. To the rest of my family thank you very much for being in my corner. Last but not least to the fans of the Farlon series enjoy. There will be a total of five books in this series. I pray that you would devour them all like a fresh fruit.

It has been a while since I wrote in this journal. This is the only way I get to express myself while I'm alone in this dungeon. My name is Olof, of the tribe Xenon, from the village Pasqual. It has been a very lonely time in this prison. All I do is write in my journal, sit and think about my past, or read from a book that was given to me by Tiris, one of the guards, entitled "The Poems of the Lion." Schracton, one of the elders from my village, wrote it.

Tiris is a good man who always looks out for me, often bringing me a loaf of bread when no one else has. One day I was very hungry. I hadn't eaten in four days and had very little water. Tiris came and opened my cell to give me some bread. As I reached out to take it, he pulled his hand away.

"Here, you need this more than any food I can give you," he said, then handed me the book of poems. I read it whenever my anger and frustration seems to be getting the best of me. The poems are really neat. I like to copy portions of them in my journal, like this one.

How long will one man walk in darkness,

When light has been revealed to him?

I can easily tell that today is the New Year because of the noise of my people above ground celebrating. I can hear them, but they can't hear me. I have been locked in this dungeon for twenty years now, punished for a horrible crime that I didn't commit. It still brings tears to my eyes as I recall the event.

When I was twelve years old, my Uncle Roland was my idol. I always looked up to him. He was one of the members of the Xenon army, an expert in sword fighting, archery, and hand-to-hand combat. He taught my friend Thomas and me all he knew. While other kids were running around the village playing, Thomas and I were constantly honing our skills. We would sneak out of our houses with our swords, bow and arrows, and a change of clothes, then spar against each other all night. I was tougher than Thomas because I always practiced to make myself better, even when he'd had enough. Wallon, the Commander-in-Chief of the Xenon army, noticed us practicing. He made us a deal that if we joined the army, our families would receive five gold coins every month. Of course, we said yes immediately because our families were poor and needed the money.

At twelve years of age, we were the youngest ever to join the Xenon army, although we were too young to fight in the war – you had to be sixteen years old. Our people consisted of twelve tribes and we were engaged in a bloody war with other tribes. Each of the twelve tribes had its own army, but when we all came together, we were called the "Fighting Eagles." For centuries we had been fighting against the Dark Wolves, a band of renegades who were committed to destroying all of our tribes, but they hadn't succeeded yet.

When Thomas and I finally turned sixteen years old, we were sent into battle. We had trained day and night for four years and now we faced the enemy for the first time. What a costly battle it was. Our unit had three hundred men and in the first month of fighting we lost eighty men, many of whom I'd grown close to because we talked a lot and told each other our deepest fears.

One night while we were sleeping, our unit was ambushed by a hundred of the Dark Wolves' finest men. Although we outnumbered them, we suffered a severe beating. Lexon, one of the Dark Wolves' generals, led the attack. He ran into our camp swinging his sword and killed five of our men in mere minutes. Some of our soldiers fled from Lexon as he came toward them. In the thick of the conflict, our men were dropping like flies. Lexon had cornered me in the Parthon Forest. I had nowhere to run. I was scared of him and he knew it.

Lexon approached me slowly. "Well, well, a young man in the army. You should have stayed with your mother."

Our swords clashed for the first time and I fell to the ground. He swung his sword for the finishing blow, but luckily I moved away, grabbed my sword, and jumped to my feet. In the midst of our sword fight, he punched me in the face. I was no match for him. I knew he would kill me sooner or later. Lexon proved to be a lot stronger than he looked as he threw me against a tree. He swung his sword to cut off my head off, but once again I was able to move out of the way and cut his left arm with my sword. The tide had changed.

I, a sixteen-year-old boy, had injured General Lexon, the strong, dominant, expert swordsman. Then I got another advantage over him when he dropped his sword after swinging it at me. I immediately pictured myself defeating him and the rest of the Dark Wolves fleeing, but that didn't happen. Instead, Lexon rushed at me, grabbed me, and threw me to the ground, then kicked me repeatedly in the face. As I gasped for air, he kicked me in the ribs and stomped on my throat. Out of fear for my life, I grabbed my dagger from its sheath on my leg and threw it at him, lodging it in his side. Lexon fell backward, screaming in pain. I managed to stand up, kicked him twice in the face, and reached for my sword. Once in hand, I charged at Lexon with all my might, my sword aimed directly at his heart.

I stopped writing and closed my journal. A primal scream escaped me, "Nooo!" Then I began to weep uncontrollably until I finally fell asleep. That night I had the dream again, the same one I'd been having for years. I was in the Talak jungle when I heard a lion roar. Out of fear I ran with all my might, hoping to not get caught by the lion. As the beast ran after me, I felt its breath as it got closer and closer. The next thing I knew, I fell in the sand as the lion moved towards me. As always, I woke up drenched in sweat, thankful that it was only a dream. The sun hadn't even come up yet. I was starving because I'd only had a small piece of chicken that the guard had given me last night. I opened up the book of poems to find something to calm me.

> *What do you fear?*
> *What troubles your soul?*
> *Does it really bother you?*
> *When your plans don't*
> *unfold?*
> *Is your greatest fear not*
> *having friends?*
> *Or watching your world*
> *come to an end?*
> *As your eyes close for the last*
> *time*
> *It's too bad that your fears*
> *have left you blind.*

Normally, I don't understand a lot of the poems, but this one I do – I know what it means. It asks the question,

'What is your fear?' and it suggests a couple of things that might make you afraid. Then it talks about how fear stops you from fully living your life. I opened up my journal and began writing again, taking up where I'd left off before sleep overcame me.

"As I charged at Lexon with all my might, I saw Thomas coming to my aid. Lexon grabbed a handful of dirt and threw it into my eyes, causing immediate pain. I rubbed them, trying to clear my vision, but I could see nothing. I grabbed what I thought was Lexon, cutting and stabbing him again and again. I heard a few cries, and then everything went silent. When I was finally able to see, Lexon was nowhere in sight and I was on top of Thomas, lying in a pool of blood. I had killed my best friend. Some of our soldiers were shocked to find that I had killed one of our comrades."

The next few months were the most horrible of my life. I was mourning the loss of my best friend and worse yet, I was tried in military court for his murder. I had no witnesses, so it was my word against theirs. My story had seemed so unbelievable, knowing that Lexon had killed twenty of our soldiers and I supposedly survived fighting him. I had no proof, my only witness was dead, and I had killed him. To this day, the incident keeps replaying in my mind, bringing forth new tears. No one believed me. Everyone felt that I had betrayed the army. I learned that the same day I killed Thomas, Uncle Roland had been killed in the same battle.

When the trial was over and I was convicted, the judge had a decision to make regarding my sentence -- either let the elders stone me to death or spend twenty years in the dungeon. I'm supposed to be released soon after serving my sentence, but was justice served? One of the poems says, *When injustice takes place, some open their mouths and some don't. Those who don't open their mouths will be justified later.*

It's amazing how I'm reminded of those poems at different times. These have truly been the worst years of my life. The only person who came to visit me was my mother. She died last year and I was not able to go to the funeral. I miss her so much. She always brought me fresh baked bread and rabbit soup. My father became an outcast after my incident and now I hear he's the town drunk. Well, the sun has come up and I anxiously await my breakfast.

The guard on duty, Borak, opened the barred door and brought me some water and a couple of eggs. "Here you go, Olof. I hear things are looking up for you."

"What do you mean?" I asked.

"You are going to have a roommate."

"Oh really?" I said, with excitement in my voice.

"Yes. They will be bringing him in a minute."

"Has King Talon said anything about me being released? You know it's been twenty years."

"I haven't heard any news. Hopefully it will be soon."

I recalled the story of a man who was supposed to be released, but the king never ordered it, so he died in the dungeon. Borak said goodbye and left. I went and stood by the door waiting for my new roommate. Maybe things were looking up for me. I never had a roommate to talk to all these years. The guards hardly talked to me at first. They viewed me as a dangerous criminal who might kill them if given the chance. I really hoped they would be letting me out soon. I heard footsteps coming down the hall. The door opened the door, a man was shoved inside and fell to the floor, and then the door closed. He was very short and skinny, five feet tall, one hundred twenty pounds.

He looked at me, then said, "Are you going to help me or just stand there looking at me?"

I quickly helped him up. "Hey, what's your name?"

"My name is Ryan. What's yours?"

"My name is Olof."

He immediately looked at me in fear and walked as far away as the confined space allowed.

"Are you the guy from the army who killed one of his own men?"

"It was an accident. I didn't mean to!"

He pressed himself against the wall, looking fearful. "Don't kill me. Why did they put me in here with a killer? I'm just a thief. Hey guards! Let me out of here!"

"I'm not a killer! I won't do anything to you."

"Guards! Guards! Help, he's going to kill me!"

"Hey, calm down in there," one of the guards said in a gruff tone.

Ryan finally calmed down and sat in the corner as far away from me as possible. The shackles on my hands and feet made me no threat to anyone. Even if I tried to fight with my hands chained together, it would be very difficult. I could barely eat with them. My feet were chained together so that I couldn't possibly run away. I quickly ate my eggs and drank my water, then watched as the rats approached looking for leftovers. The room was almost completely dark. The only source of light was from the torch in the passageway outside of the door, which shone through the bars of the small opening at eye level. There were spiders too, which caused me to become quite ill when they bit me while I was sleeping. If I want to write in my journal or read my book, I have to stay by the door to get what little light is available. I watched as Ryan grew tired and finally fell asleep. Having nothing else to do, I opened up my journal and began to write.

"Well, I have a new roommate. His name is Ryan and he is dreadfully afraid of me. I really don't blame him. Who knows all the stories he may have heard about Olof, the Terrible? I've been thinking a lot about my father lately. His name is Pereal. He makes weapons for the Xenon army. Too bad the king doesn't pay him much.

Without my father we would be unable to defend ourselves from the Dark Wolves. It seems to me that this is a losing battle for us. The Dark Wolves have killed so many of our people that I've lost count. We won a few small battles. Last year King Talon was almost killed in an assassination attempt when he was shot in the chest with an arrow. It took him two months to recover. When they let me out, I hope I can find a good job, get married, and live in peace. I might move out of the village for good because it holds too many bad memories for me. I hear one of the guards calling me now."

"Hey Olof, you've got a visitor," Borak yelled.

"Okay, let them in," I said, shocked that someone would come to visit me.

Tiris stepped through the door with a basket of food. "Hello Olof."

"How are you doing, Tiris?"

"Pretty good. How have they been treating you in here?"

"Not bad. Not much food, as you can see. I'm getting thinner and thinner by the day."

"Well, I brought you some food that my wife made. Let's see what we have here. There's some fresh baked bread, rabbit soup, and for dessert, some apple pie."

"Wow! You didn't have to do that. Thank you -- and tell your wife I said thanks a lot."

I quickly tore off a piece of bread and began eating the soup.

"Olof, my wife and I have been praying for you. Have you read any of the poems from the book I gave you?"

"I have! I've been enjoying it very much. All I do is read those poems and write in the journal you gave me. It helps get things off my chest. By the way, who is this Schracton that wrote the book?"

18

"He is the oldest living elder of all our tribes."

"How old is he?"

"I believe he is about four hundred years old. Schracton is the only prophet among our people."

"Four hundred years old? No one lives to be that old."

"Oh yes, he is. God has blessed him to live that long. You need to meet him someday."

"I would love to, hopefully when I get out of here."

"How long have you been in here now, Olof?"

"It's been twenty years."

"They should have released you by now."

"I know, but they haven't. I'm still here and I haven't heard anything from the king."

"Why don't you write him a letter? Let the king know that you have served your time. I will deliver it for you."

"Would you do that for me? I sure would appreciate that. Why have you been so nice to me? No one else cares for me, except my mother, but she's dead. Everyone else has turned their backs on me." I fell to my knees and began crying. Tiris hugged me.

"It will be okay, Olof. Don't worry, I will pray to God that you will be let out."

"Thanks a lot," I said, wiping the tears from my eyes.

"You write that letter today and I will come by and pick it up early tomorrow morning."

"Thank you so much, Tiris. I owe you."

"Don't worry about it, Olof." Tiris gave me one big hug before being escorted out by two guards.

* * * * *

Serpentine, the six-foot four-inch, two hundred pound evil leader with two heads -- one the head of a deformed man, the other the head of a serpent, stood up from the table and paced around the room.

"There are twelve tribes in the land of Farlon. We have one hundred thousand soldiers. They have a population of three million, with only five hundred thousand soldiers in their army. We are stronger than they are, so why is it that we have not completely wiped out even one of their tribes? All we need to do is destroy one tribe and this will stop the prophecy, but it seems we cannot even do that."

Golan interrupted. "Master, it is not as easy as it looks."

Serpentine picked up Golan and threw him across the room. "What do you mean it's not that easy? We have the upper hand on them. All we need to do is wipe out one tribe. The smallest tribe is Xenon. What we need to do is launch an all-out assault against that one tribe. Here's my plan. Lexon, you will take your troops and invade their village. Slaughter every man, woman, and child. Those that flee for their lives will meet the rest of our army at the outskirts of the village."

Tarlenum whispered, "But their army will be on the lookout for any invasion."

"True," Serpentine responded, "but we will surprise them. We shall go at night. Their soldiers will find it hard to stay awake at that time. Lexon, once your troops are finished, burn the village to the ground!"

"Yes, Master. Your wish is my command," Lexon responded with a wicked smile.

All of the generals walked out of the room after Serpentine dismissed them.

* * * * *

"Your majesty, King Talon,

My name is Olof. I am a simple

servant of your kingdom. I have been

imprisoned in the Carlyle dungeon for twenty years for the accidental death of my friend, Thomas, during a battle against the Dark Wolves. I faithfully served with the Fighting Eagles for four years before this incident. I have finally served my sentence and I now await your permission for me to be released. Since I've been incarcerated, my mother died. All I have left are my two brothers, Syphon and Phlax, my sister, Orion, and my father, Pereal. I long to see them. I am sorry for the grief that I have caused the kingdom. Once I get myself situated after my release, one month later I will leave the land of Farlon forever. All I ask is that I be set free from this God-forsaken place.

Thank you,

Olof"

The next morning I woke up bright and early to find Ryan devouring some of my bread. Borak yelled through the door, "Olof you have a visitor!"

The door opened. Tiris had returned as promised. "Good morning, Olof, and good morning to you, too," he said, looking at Ryan. Ryan grabbed his bread and moved away, not saying a word.

"Tiris, I have that letter ready for you to deliver."

"Good! I will deliver it right away. Did you sleep well?"

"It's hard sleeping on a floor of rocks, but I'm used to it. I can't complain, at least I didn't get bitten by a spider last night."

"You will be out in no time, Olof. Don't worry about it. Do you have a place to stay when you get out?"

"No, I don't. I guess I will sleep wherever I can."

"I tell you what, when you get out, I will let you stay at my place with me and my wife."

"Do you really mean it? This is so nice of you. How can I ever repay you?"

"Don't worry about it. I will ride up to the king's castle today. Hopefully you will hear from the king soon."

"The king will not respond to you. You are a murderer. Olof. You are going to rot in this dungeon," Ryan yelled.

"Don't listen to him, Olof. You must believe."

"Why would the king listen to me anyway? I'm just a prisoner."

"Olof, you've got to have faith."

"Why don't you just get out of here with that nonsense?" Ryan yelled again, more vehemently this time.

"Trust me, Olof, you will hear from the king. God will see to it." Tiris left the dungeon escorted by Borak, the guard.

* * * * *

Well, it's been two weeks and I haven't heard from the king. Maybe Ryan was right. I am just a peasant in prison. Why would the king read my letter? Who am I? Tiris hasn't been back to visit me. He might have given up on me, too. I'll bet he doesn't want anything to do with me as well. Ryan got released yesterday and hopefully he learned his lesson. I must go; the guards are calling my name.

The door opened and Borak entered. "You have to get cleaned up, Olof."

"Why is that?"

"You are about to go see the king. He has summoned you to come and talk with him. He is in the other room."

I quickly ran, got showered, shaved, and put on the clean clothes the guards gave me, then I walked into the room where the king was. When I saw him, I bowed and put my face to the ground.

"Your majesty, how are you?"

"I am great. You can get off the floor now, Olof."

I immediately stood on my feet, yet kept my eyes facing the ground. I nervously said, "So why have you come here, my Lord?"

"Are you a man, Olof?"

"What did you say?"

"I said, are you a man, Olof?"

"Yes, Your Majesty."

"Then look me in the eye, Olof...face to face." The king lifted my chin until we made eye contact.

"I think you know why I am here, Olof. I received your letter. Tiris, the guard delivered it. He had a lot of good things to say about you. Tiris said that if you were to be released, you would be in his care. Is that correct?"

"That is true, Your Highness."

"I enjoyed your letter. You don't seem like a troublemaker or a murderer, but looks can be deceiving. I have a proposition for you, Olof."

"Go ahead, Your Majesty."

"As of today you are a free man. You can gather up all of your things; however, if you get into any trouble, you will be put back into the dungeon for the rest of your life."

I was so happy that I ran to hug the king, but he held me back and just shook my hand.

"I believe you will do well, Olof. I think you have learned your lesson."

"Oh thank you, thank you, King Talon. You will not regret your decision."

I ran out of the room. Tears of joy were streaming down my face as I went back to the dungeon to gather my belongings. After I grabbed my things, I was escorted out of the prison to a waiting carriage. Once inside, we were off to the village Pasqual, home of the Xenonites. I opened my journal to express my joy.

"I have finally been released from the dark dungeon abode of the rats and spiders. I can't believe it. It seems like a dream. I hope no one wakes me up. Twenty years of being away from home. I wonder how my father is doing. Phlax is forty, Syphon is thirty-eight, and my little sister, Orion, is thirty-two. Time really does fly. We have passed through the Talak jungle, which is still as beautiful as ever. I saw two lions and a snake. Now we are approaching the Parthon forest. Once we go through this forest, I will be home. I will find a wife, a good job, and I will live happily ever after watching birds fly by and land on the branches of these huge oak trees.

We finally reached the village Pasqual. A lot had changed. The village had extended while I was locked up. There's the meat market. I see the prices are too high for me. I beheld couples walking by holding hands. The bar was still in the center of the village. The old church was still standing after all these years. The carriage stopped. I had arrived at Tiris's house.

I grabbed my things, said goodbye to the carriage driver, and then ran to hug Tiris and his wife who were waiting outside for me.

"Hey Olof, this is my wife, Susan."

"Glad to meet you. I'm Olof."

"It's nice to meet you, Olof. Let me leave so you men can talk. I need to finish dinner. I'll see you in a minute." Susan walked back inside to finish preparing the meal.

"You are looking good, Olof. I'll bet you're glad to be out of there."

"If I didn't leave when I did, the rats would have kicked me out anyway." Both of us chuckled at the thought of that.

"Tiris, I am sorry to be a burden. I was just wondering if you had a copper coin so I could get a drink from the bar."

"I can't support that bad habit, Olof. I believe in God. You are going to have to get your own money for that. By the way, you can't be doing that while you're sleeping at my house. We have rules here."

"I understand, Tiris. You don't have to preach to me. So what's for dinner?"

"Were having fish tonight. I caught some trout earlier at Lake Marsh."

"I haven't had fish in over twenty years."

"Well, get ready, there's plenty of it."

I went to wash my hands, then sat down at the dinner table. There were at least ten pieces of fish, corn, a loaf of bread, and a cherry pie.

"It's been awhile since I sat at a dinner table and had a meal with a family," I said as I grabbed some fish.

"Well, there's plenty more, Olof," Susan said, smiling.

"So Olof, are you going to see how your family is doing?" Tiris asked.

"Definitely, right after I finish my dinner I'm going to see how my father is doing," I replied.

"Well, what about a job? Do you have any idea of what kind of work you plan on doing?" Susan asked.

"I'm going to see if I can get a job working with my father making weapons for the army. It pays pretty decent now," I said excitedly. "By the way, Tiris, can you take me to see Schracton tomorrow?"

"No problem. It will be bright and early in the morning because after I take you, I have to go to the castle and talk with the king."

"What about?" I asked.

"Because the king is considering hiring me as one of the royal guards."

"That means you will be living in the castle if he hires you. I think you will definitely get the job."

"Well, there are over one thousand people with much more experience than I have trying to get the same job."

"How much will they pay you, Tiris?" I asked in curiosity.

"One gold coin per day."

"Wow! Thirty gold coins a month for guarding the king. Where can I sign up?"

"Sorry, Olof, the king doesn't hire anyone who has been in the dungeon before. You can't even be a cook for him if you have been tried and convicted for a crime."

"Well, that's okay. I think I will do pretty well at my father's job. You know they had me doing that in the dungeon for the first ten years I was there."

After we were finished eating, I said goodbye to Tiris and Susan and left to see how my father was doing.

As I walked through the village, a lot of people gave me evil looks. Some of them noticed my prison marks on my arms. The guards had branded an "X" on my left and right shoulders to show that I was a convicted murderer. One guy walked past me and said hello. I greeted him with a hello, but kept walking.

I finally made it to my father's house and knocked on the door. My father, Pereal, answered the door in no time, holding a drink in his hand. Once he realized who I was, he dropped his mug. It broke and spilled its contents all over the floor. Then he gave me a big hug.

"My boy is at home at last. So when did you get out? I see you lost some weight. Have you seen your brothers and your sister? Where are you staying?"

"One question at a time. I got out today. No, I haven't seen Syphon, Phlax, or Orion. Yes, I lost some weight. I am staying with a friend of mine named Tiris."

"Have you eaten already?"

"Yes. I had some fish at Tiris's house."

"So what are your plans now?"

"Well, I was hoping to get a job with you, if you would talk to your boss and see if he will hire me."

"Sorry, son, he will not hire a convicted criminal, but maybe there are other jobs you could get."

"Well, I don't know how to do anything else. My trade in prison was making weapons."

"Let's not worry about that right now, Olof. I'm just glad to see you back."

"Where are Syphon, Phlax, and Orion?"

"They still live here in the village, except for Orion. She got married to a Volorite and she lives in the village Harlon. She has three children. Phlax and Syphon are both married and they each have one child. In fact, they should be here in a few minutes. We're about to go to the bar. Do you want to come along?"

"Well, uh, I don't know," I replied, thinking about what Tiris said.

"Come on, son. They haven't seen you in twenty years. You need to spend some time with your family."

"Well, I guess I'll go for a short while."

Phlax and Syphon walked into the house and saw me talking with our father. Phlax picked me up, and gave me such a big hug, I could barely breathe.

"My little brother is home at last," Phlax said, tears forming in his eyes.

"Looks like you've put on a lot of weight, Phlax. What are you now, seven feet tall, five hundred pounds?"

"Close. I am seven feet, four hundred fifty pounds -- all fat, no muscle." Both of us laughed.

Syphon said, "Hello, Olof, nice to see you." He didn't hug me or shake my hand. "You know you killed Momma. She died of a broken heart because her baby boy was locked up in the dungeon. That's why I didn't come to visit you -- because you killed her!"

"You say it again and I will knock you out," I said, my fists clinched in anger.

Syphon punched me and knocked me through the door. Others from the village gathered around to watch us fight. Syphon was five feet eleven inches, three hundred pounds, and all muscle. I was six feet, one hundred ninety pounds. He had an advantage over me. Syphon swung again, but this time he missed and I punched him in his ribs. I kicked his leg as hard as I could and he fell to the ground. Syphon got up, grabbed me, and threw me to the ground. I quickly got up and punched him about four times in the face. Siphon swung again, but I avoided it and hit him in the stomach. The fight was on. Roland had taught me well. I punched Syphon again, bloodying his nose. A few of the villagers, including Tiris, came and broke up the fight. Syphon just walked off in anger and frustration, holding his nose.

Tiris yanked me off to the side, away from everyone else. "Olof, what do you think you're doing? Do you realize you could end up in the dungeon for this? What were you thinking?"

"You don't know what he said to me!"

"It doesn't matter. You can't just lose your temper whenever someone says something to you."

"But you didn't hear what he said to me!"

"Well, tell me, what did he say?"

"He said that I am the reason my mother died." I started to cry and ran out of the village. Tiris called after me, telling me to come back. When I'd made it to the Parthon forest, I sat on a big rock, pulled out my journal, and began to write.

"What Syphon said to me really hurt me. How could he say that? I know that he was hurt just as much as I was when Momma died. I was never the same after she passed away. I guess Syphon wasn't either. Tiris was right. I shouldn't have been out there fighting Syphon. Well, I guess he said just the right thing to tick me off. My life is horrible. Who am I fooling? They should just call me 'Olof, the Terrible.' Why, I can't even get a job. I'm always relying on someone else. Who would want to marry me if I don't have a job? What good am I? I feel so worthless. I know what I'm going to do, I'll just grab my clothes and leave this village for good."

I closed my journal and quickly walked to Tiris's house. It was obvious he'd been waiting for me outside.

"I was wondering if you were going to come back."

"Well, it's just for a minute. I'm grabbing my clothes and leaving this village. It has nothing but bad memories for me."

"It's only what you make it, Olof."

"What do you mean by that?"

"It's only what you make it. I don't believe you were expecting anything better and now you're about to call it quits and leave the village forever. Are you going to be a quitter for the rest of your life? Go ahead, the choice is yours. Do you know what I would do if I were you?"

"What's that?"

"Why don't you just sleep on it for tonight and when you wake up, go visit Schracton tomorrow morning."

"Maybe you're right. I might feel a little better in the morning after a good night's sleep."

I took Tiris's advice and went inside his house to get some sleep.

* * * * *

The next morning, Tiris woke me up bright and early to go visit Schracton. He handed me an orange and told me to get dressed. After I got dressed, we were off. We talked along the way and I got a lot of things off my chest. I felt Tiris was becoming a close friend I never had. He seemed to take the place of Thomas. I always told Thomas everything that was going on in my life. We finally made it to the Gail River.

"So, are we there yet?"

"Not yet."

"What do you mean 'not yet?' We can't swim across this river."

"I know that's what the ferryboat is for. The man on board will take you the rest of the way."

"Hey Billy, can you take my friend Olof to the island Granoy to see the prophet Schracton?"

"No problem," Billy said. "Come on board, Olof."

Tiris handed Billy a copper coin and said goodbye. I watched Tiris head towards the royal castle. Once I got on board, I sat down and enjoyed the scenery. I opened up my journal to write.

"I wonder about this Schracton. I've heard nothing but good things. Is he really a prophet? Well, I guess I'll find out. My hands are swollen from fighting my brother yesterday. When I get back, I'm going to find Syphon and tell him that I'm sorry for what happened. First, though, if Tiris says I need to see Schracton, then I guess I do."

I put my journal away and started a conversation with Billy. "So, how long have you been driving the ferryboat?"

"For two hundred years I have been taking people to see Schracton. I have even taken the king to see him a few times."

"The king goes to visit him as well?"

"Yes, he does. Schracton is full of wisdom. You will enjoy his presence. Trust me, you will never be the same after talking with him."

"Really? What else can you tell me about him?"

"Time is up, young lad. You will see for yourself. We have just arrived at Schracton's home."

I looked at the island and saw there was just one big cave surrounded by trees. After saying goodbye to the ferryman, I climbed out of the boat and walked towards the cave.

"Are you going into my cave without my permission, Olof?" I heard a voice ask.

I turned around to see an old man about five feet five inches, one hundred pounds, walking with a large staff that was taller than him. The staff kept changing into a snake, then back to a wooden staff. I was so shocked by that I couldn't say a word.

"Well, how are you today, Olof?"

"How did you know my name?"

"God told me."

As the old man entered the dark cave, it lit up as if a bright light had been turned on.

"How did you do that?"

"When light walks into darkness, the darkness turns to light."

"I've wanted to meet you ever since I read the book you wrote, *The Poems of the Lion*. That book is excellent. I have almost finished reading it."

"After you are done, you need to read it over and over again until you die because you can never be finished with that book."

"So you are Schracton?"

"I think you already knew that. So tell me, Olof, why do you call yourself Olof, the Terrible?"

"How did you know that?"

"I already told you, I know things. Now answer the question. Why do you call yourself Olof the Terrible?"

"Because I always have bad things happen to me. It's like I bring trouble everywhere I go."

"That's not what God calls you. He calls you Olof the Great because God is going to use your life like never

44

before. From this day forward, your life will never be the same."

"Why does God want to use my life?"

"God chose you. He picks and chooses whomever He wants to. You are going to lead your people to victory over the Dark Wolves. Stop focusing on the past and good things will happen. The dreams you have been having about a lion chasing you… the lion is God and you have been running from Him all your life. Olof, you must surrender to God and ask him to forgive your sins." I felt as if Schracton looked right through my eyes into the depths of my soul.

"Olof, I have a few things to give you before you leave. This is the Sword of Judah. It is only of value to a man or woman of good character. Next is another book that I wrote, *The Power That Is Within You.*" The very last thing is a bow and arrow. Trust me, you will need this sooner than you think. Now, young Olof, it is time for you to go.

By the way, give this gold coin to Billy. Olof, you have had this on your mind since you first saw me, so let me tell you -- I am four hundred fifty years old. You can stop guessing."

I gave Schracton a hug and said goodbye. I left the cave and hurried to the waiting ferryboat. As I walked to river, I looked at the Sword of Judah. It was a double-edged sword. The blade was made of pure gold. It was the first time I had ever seen a double-edged sword. A scripture was engraved on the handle, Hebrews 4:12.

"For the word of God is quick, and powerful, and sharper than any two-edged sword, piercing even to the dividing asunder of soul and spirit, and of the joints and marrow, and is a discerner of the thoughts and intents of the heart."

"I'm back, Billy," I said, handing him the gold coin. It was nearly dark as we sailed across the river. We didn't speak at all. Truly, I was still in shock from the

46

conversation I'd had with Schracton. I couldn't wait to tell Tiris what had happened.

We finally made it to land and I got out of the ferryboat. The moon was shining bright, even though it was pitch dark. I began to think about what Schracton said, about me asking God for forgiveness. I fell to my knees and said, "God, I am sorry for all the wrong I have done. I need you to forgive me of my sins." After thinking about it all, I began to cry. I felt clean. I felt relief. I felt forgiven. Billy said I would never be the same again after talking to Schracton.

Next thing I heard was a lot of horses coming down the road. I hid myself in the bushes and watched them ride by. To my shock it wasn't the king's men or any of our soldiers, it was the Dark Wolves and they were headed towards our village. I ran as fast as I could to warn the others, but I couldn't outrun the horses so I prayed, "God, please don't let anything happen to my family."

As I ran towards the village, I began to notice some Dark Wolves just outside of the village with weapons in hand while those on horseback invaded, torches in hand. *Oh my goodness, they planned to burn down the village*! I grabbed my bow and arrow and shot a couple of them. Another soldier noticed me and shouted, "One of the Xenonites is here. Let's get him!"

I pulled out the Sword of Judah to defend myself. As I swung the sword, I knocked two of them down. I knew there was no time to waste; I had to get to the village to help the others before it was too late. I saw people being killed by the dozens and houses going up in flames. Upon entering the village, I noticed Lexon wielding a big club.

My father was in the center of the village yelling, "Run to the tunnels!"

What is he talking about? I wondered. Lexon rode up on his horse and hit my father in the face with a club.

Blood poured from my father's head as he fell to the ground.

"NOOO!" I screamed. "I'll make you pay for that!"

Lexon turned around. His eyes came to rest on me. "Well, well, if it isn't the little boy I fought years ago. Now he has become a man and he has the Sword of Judah. It will do you no good against a fighter like me."

Our clashing of swords sounded like thunder. After all these years, I was still no match for him. Lexon got off his horse. "I admire your bravery because the rest of your army is afraid of me."

I swung my sword. Lexon caught it with one hand and took it from me, then kicked me in the face. Once I recovered from my head spinning, I swung at Lexon with all my might. He caught my left hand and squeezed it until it broke. As I fell backward, he punched me in the face, knocking me to the ground.

When I looked up I saw a soldier from our army fighting Lexon. He looked at me and said, "Run for your life. Go to the tunnels!"

I couldn't leave without the Sword of Judah, so I grabbed my bow and arrow and shot Lexon twice in the back. I watched him as he fell down. The sword flew out of his hand and landed in the dirt. Quickly, I grabbed it, and then ran to my father.

"Father, get up, get up! You can't die on me now," I said as I shook his lifeless body.

The soldier who had saved my life grabbed me by the arm. "I must get you to the tunnels. Follow me."

We ran inside of a hut that was aflame. He showed me the opening in the floor that led to the tunnels. "Go! You must follow the tunnels out of here."

"But what about you?" I asked.

"Don't worry about me. If I die with my people, then I die."

I ran through the tunnel crying. My father was dead and my brothers probably were too.

Lexon got up off the ground slowly, and then yelled, "Men, burn this village to the ground. Let no one escape!"

The Dark Wolves continued their slaughter, burning the whole village to the ground. As I ran through the tunnel, I heard voices up ahead. I didn't know who it was, so I pulled out my sword as I approached. There were twenty other Xenonites from my village. Some of them had been burned, some wounded by swords.

"Who are you?" one of them asked me.

"My name is Olof. What is your name?"

"My name is Balsk. What household are you from?"

"My father is Pereal. I have two brothers, Phlax and Syphon, and one sister, Orion."

"You're the one who just got out of the dungeon." When Balsk said that, everyone moved away from me out of fear.

"Let me introduce you to everyone. My daughter Makka, Rinu, Joles, Vine, Hoi, Dranu, Cantu, Walas, Vil, Knost, Celon, Karas, Jamgu, Glotus, Ari, Mosta, Lean, Whilt, and Sho."

I looked at Balsk in amazement, thinking that all of them were his children. "Nice to meet you. I'm Olof." I thought to myself, *twenty guys, one girl, and an army of thousands looking for us. We're going to die.* I sat in the corner and pulled out my journal to write.

"Well, God, I really don't understand. My father is dead and probably my brothers are too. It's pretty frustrating when no one wants to be around me. I didn't get a chance to spend any time with my

family.

Olof, the Terrible"

* * * * *

Serpentine asked, "So how did the battle go,

Lexon?"

"It went very well, Master. Thousands were killed.

We burned the entire village to the ground."

"Did any escape?"

"Some did escape, Master Serpentine."

"You got that right! One hundred people escaped! I

should have your head for that!"

"I'm sorry, Master. We will search and destroy

those remaining one hundred."

"You'd better. That promised seed is among them.

Destroy the rest of those people, get the Sword of Judah,

and kill its owner. You had two chances to kill him and

failed both times. Because of you, that boy lived to become a man and now he's becoming a thorn in my side!"

"Yes, Master."

King Talon spoke. "The reason for this meeting is a matter of grave importance. The village of Pasqual was burned down and many lives were lost. I need five volunteers to search the tunnels for survivors and protect every last one of them."

"But that means the castle will be unprotected with only five royal guards here with you, Sire," Lotus spoke up.

"Not true, Lotus. I still have those five plus one thousand troops that surround the castle. I desperately need five of you to go and find my people. If that tribe is completely destroyed, the prophecy will not be fulfilled. My life is not that important. I can be replaced. The chosen ones are destined to come. One from each tribe will come forth and bring an end to the Dark Wolves. The five of you who volunteer are to treat those people like royalty. Protect them to the end, even if it costs your own life. Now, which five of you will come forward to accept this challenge?"

Five men stepped forward. Nolan, Shaw, Lotus, War, and Regal stood before the king, swords in hand. "I need you five to find the survivors and deliver this food. If they need anything else, make sure they get it," said King Talon.

The soldiers mounted their horses and rode away.

Meanwhile, back in the tunnels, I was seated, wrapping my broken hand when Dranu walked up. "What happened to your hand?"

"I broke it fighting Lexon."

"You should be glad that was the only thing broken. Not many people fight Lexon and live to tell about it."

"Yes, that's what I hear, but trust me, I'm going to get him. He killed my father when the Dark Wolves invaded the village."

"Trust me, you don't want to fight Lexon. He has killed some of our best troops. What's your name again?"

"Olof. What's yours?"

"Dranu."

"So Dranu, are all of you related?"

"No. The only ones related are Balsk and his daughter, Makka."

"Is any of your family still alive?"

"I'm afraid not. Those monsters slaughtered my whole family! How about you?"

"My father is dead, but I don't know about my brothers."

"Well, I hope they're still alive because it's rough being all alone."

"Do you think we're safe down here?"

"Only temporarily, Olof. The Dark Wolves will not stop until they have destroyed us all." Dranu paused and looked down at Olof's sword. "How did you get the Sword of Judah?"

"Schracton the Prophet gave it to me. That reminds me, I wonder if he is still alive?"

"Trust me, Olof, if Schracton was dead, you'd know about it. The Prophet is alive and well."

"My hand is broken and I'm starving. What I wouldn't do for a roasted chicken right now."

"We'll get some food soon. These tunnels lead to the other villages."

"Well, maybe I'll get to see Orion."

"Who's Orion? Your wife-to-be?"

"No, she's my sister. She got married and moved to the village Harlon."

"Well, at least her village isn't in danger yet, but you never know with the Dark Wolves. So tell me, how did you survive Lexon?"

"Well, to be honest, I got lucky. While I was fighting him, one of the royal guards saved my life."

"Well, I guess we'd better get some rest because we have a lot of traveling to do tomorrow."

"Sounds good. I'll see you in the morning, Dranu."

"Have a good night, Olof."

* * * * *

When I awoke the next morning, I had a lot of pain in my left hand. I wanted to cry it was so bad. I heard people walking through the tunnel towards us. I grabbed the sword of Judah in fear that it might be the Dark Wolves.

"No need to grab weapons, we are Xenonites," a male voice said.

Once they came stepped from the dark tunnel, I saw they were telling the truth. When Balsk noticed the man and woman, he embraced them.

"I thought you guys didn't make it," Balsk said, choked with emotion, tears falling down his face.

I quickly stood up to introduce myself. "My name is Olof. What's yours?"

The woman spoke first. "I'm Tira and this is my husband, Garl."

"Nice to meet you," I said.

Garl cleared his throat. "We have a big problem. There's an older man with us who is wounded. My wife and I have been carrying him since we found him lying unconscious in the village. We need your help. He is in no condition to walk and he has a bad head wound."

"Where is he?" inquired Balsk. "We have plenty of men who can carry him."

"He is down the tunnel, not too far from here," Garl replied. He looked exhausted.

We all ran to help the older man. I couldn't believe my eyes. "Father, you're alive!

Pereal looked up. "Olof, my boy. You're alive. I wondered what happened to you." I hugged him for a long time. It seemed like an eternity since I'd last seen him.

Balsk interrupted. "Olof, you have to let him go. We must carry him to the next village and find a doctor because that cut on his head looks pretty bad."

I volunteered to be the first one to carry my father.

King Talon was pacing back and forth while his wife Selena laid reading in bed. "Why are you not in bed yet, my king?"

"I will be in a minute. I can't sleep."

"It seems you have a lot on your mind. You must realize that God is going to take care of everything. Don't let this war trouble you."

"I can't stop thinking about the many lives lost. I don't know if the five royal guards I sent to look for survivors are okay... and what if Serpentine is planning another attack?"

"You have your soldiers surrounding the outskirts of every village, swords in hand, ready for battle. What else can you do?"

"Well, I guess you're right. Is our son Grace asleep already?"

"I believe so," she said, but with a note of uncertainty in her voice.

"He is going to make a fine king someday," Talon said confidently.

"Yes, he will, Talon. Now come on, let's get some rest."

"In a minute. I'm going to have one of the servants bring me some fresh apple juice."

Selena turned away and immediately fell asleep. King Talon walked to the door to speak to his royal guardsman, Ox.

"Do you need anything, Sire?"

"Yes. Could you please have one of the servants bring me some freshly squeezed apple juice?"

"Of course. It will be right up."

While King Talon waited, he prayed. "God, we need your help. You see everything that is taking place. We are outnumbered and many soldiers are dying. I hope the chosen ones are coming soon because we are fighting a losing battle. Time is running out. Please give me wisdom at this time to make good decisions for the benefit of Your people."

His prayers were interrupted by a knock at the door. The king opened it to see his servant, Rotham, holding a pitcher of apple juice.

"Where is Ox?" the king asked.

"I don't know, Sire. I'm was told to bring the juice you requested."

"Okay, now take a drink of it, Rotham," the king instructed in a calm voice.

Rotham grabbed the pitcher and drank from it slowly.

"Well, I see it's not poison," said the king. He took the pitcher and drank from it.

Immediately, two guards came running up the stairs, shouting in panic, "King Talon! King Talon! Something is wrong! We found Rotham tied up in the courtyard!"

The king turned to look at the man he thought was Rotham and watched as he transformed into Malgrim.

Malgrim whispered in the king's ear, "Long die the king."

The words had barely crossed his lips when the king fell to the floor dead. Malgrim grabbed Queen Selena by the arm. Although she struggled with all her might, Malgrim dragged her to the balcony where a large raven was waiting and carried them both away before the guards made it to the top of the stairs to stop him. Malgrim's evil laugh was heard as they flew away.

Daqual, one of the royal guards, went to rouse 12-year old Prince Grace from his slumber.

While wiping the sleep from his eyes, Grace asked, "What's the meaning of this Daqual?"

"I'm sorry, Your Highness, but terrible things have taken place while you were asleep."

"What happened?"

"Your father, the king, has been poisoned. He is dead. Your mother was taken captive by one of the Dark

Wolves. Your coronation must take place immediately before the people begin to worry."

"I must go and speak to Schracton right away. He will know what I should do."

"It is not safe for you to leave the castle. I will bring Schracton here. The other three guards will protect you while I'm gone."

"There are supposed to be four. Where is the other guard?"

"I forgot to mention the royal guard, Ox, was killed during this incident. Your Majesty, I suggest that you not leave your room for the time being. Your life is in danger and we can't afford to lose you because then we would have no king."

"Calm down, Daqual! I need you to bring Schracton here at once and we will work out the details later."

"Yes, Your Majesty."

Daqual quickly left the castle on horseback to get Schracton.

* * * * *

As we made our way through the tunnels towards the other village, we were greeted by one of the royal guards.

"Hello, my name is Nolan. I am one of the king's royal guards. I was sent here to protect you by order of King Talon himself," Nolan said.

I was in shock. Nolan was the guard who'd saved my life while I was fighting Lexon. I wondered if he remembered me.

"How is King Talon?" Jamgu asked.

"The king has been killed and the Dark Wolves have captured Queen Selena."

"What's going to happen now? Who will be king?" I asked.

"Prince Grace, King Talon's only child will become king, I'm sure," Nolan responded.

"Shouldn't you be at the castle protecting the little boy?" asked Garl with a grimace.

Nolan threw Garl against the side of the tunnel, pulled out his dagger, and put it to Garl's throat. "Watch your tongue, young man, before I cut it off. No one speaks against royalty and gets away with it!"

"So what are the plans?" Balsk asked as he separated the two of them.

"My plan is this -- we need to get all of you over to the Frilch village. From there we will get a doctor for this one." He pointed to Pereal. "I also have three hundred of our finest soldiers protecting that village and willing to die for it."

We continued walking until we grew tired and decided to stop and rest for the night. That night I had a dream about the lion again. I sat in the grass talking to him.

"Why do you keep calling yourself 'Olof the Terrible' when I call you 'Olof the Great?'"

"That's how I feel at times," I told him.

"So everyday when you're not feeling good, this is what you are going to say about yourself?"

"Well, I guess."

"I have called you to be a blessing to your people. I am going to use your life like never before. You will be an encouragement to all."

"When will this take place?"

"In time. Right now you are in preparation. What you need to be doing is talking to me in prayer and getting to know me by reading those two books -- *The Poems of the Lion* and *The Power Within You*. Both of them will teach you a lot. One more thing, you need to start fasting."

"What is fasting?"

"Fasting is when you deny yourself food for spiritual purposes. You see, Olof, the closer you get to me, the more the Sword of Judah will become a blessing to you. Why, you haven't seen even half of its power yet. There's a scripture that says, 'Blessed are the pure in heart for they shall see God.' What you need to do is get closer to me, Olof."

"It all makes sense now. You are God and at first I was running from you."

"Yes, you were, Olof, but then you let me catch you in the end."

"How do I defeat the Dark Wolves?"

"By staying close to me because they are afraid of me. As I manifest myself to you more and more, they will fear you."

"Thank you, God. I love you."

"I love you too, Olof, very much. Many people you will meet will teach you a lot, but you must be willing to learn, Olof."

As God turned and walked away, I awoke from my sleep. I prayed until the sun rose and beamed sunlight into the tunnel. Today was the day I decided to fast. I sat down and read from both of my books until everyone else woke up.

* * * * *

"Well, hello there, young Grace. What can I assist you with?"

"I am only twelve years old. My mother is being held captive, a war is raging, and we are losing. This burden is all on me!"

"Young Grace, do you remember your father?"

"Of course I do, Schracton. Why do you ask?"

"Well, if you knew your father, you would imitate him. He was a man of prayer and that is what you need to be. You called me to give you advice on these situations, but I will not give you any. Young Grace, you must seek God in prayer and allow him to show you what you must do. I must be going now. By the way, there is a raven on your balcony with a note from Serpentine to offer a deal to you for the freedom of your mother. Decisions... decisions for which you must pray to find answers." Schracton walked out of the room.

Grace ran to the balcony. Sure enough, there was a raven there with a note tied to his leg. Grace opened it up and read it:

"Dear Prince,

It seems your kingdom is in trouble. You are definitely not a strong man like your father was. You are just a boy. Let me get right to the point. I will stop warring with you for the rest of your life and I will return your mother to you if you will abide by my terms. I want the remaining one hundred Xenonites brought to me within two days. I will be sending Lexon, one of my

generals, to talk with you tomorrow to

discuss this peace treaty. If you do not listen,

you and your kingdom will be destroyed.

Your mother will be first."

Serpentine

King Grace quickly called Nile to his room.

"What is it, your Majesty?"

"I need you to announce to all the tribes that my

coronation will take place tonight. I must officially take the

throne right away. I need you to get Schracton. I want him

to speak to the people tonight."

"Yes, Sire. I will take care of everything right away.

I will also have some food prepared for everyone

attending."

"Thank you, Nile. Tell everyone that I don't want to be disturbed until tonight, not even for a meal. I'll eat after the coronation ceremony."

Nile left and King Grace spent the rest of the day in prayer.

* * * * *

As soon as we made it through the tunnel and finally arrived at Frilch village, we left my father with the doctor.

Nolan said, "We must be leaving now to go to the castle for the coronation of King Grace. We will come back later to check on Pereal."

We followed his orders and made our way to the royal castle. There was food from all over the world. It was the biggest party I had ever seen. I looked around to see if I could find Orion, but there were too many people.

Nolan looked at me. "How did you learn to fight like that?"

"Well, I was in the army four years before I was put in prison."

"I have never seen anyone stand up to Lexon like that. You definitely have courage and boldness. Who trained you in the army?"

"Roland."

"You knew Roland? I heard plenty of good things about him and his heroic deeds. There's a statue of him in this castle honoring him."

"He was my uncle. I didn't know there was a statue of him. I would like to see it. Can you take me?"

"Sorry, Olof, only people who work in the castle are blessed to see anything inside of it."

I felt disappointed, but said nothing. I decided to get some food and drink. As I was pouring myself some juice, I saw Schracton stand to speak. He waited until the crowd was quiet before he began.

"People of the land of Farlon, we have had some terrible things happen recently. Our beloved King Talon was poisoned and died suddenly. His wife, Queen Selena, has been taken captive by the enemy, but as a people, we need not fear because God says, 'When the enemy shall come in like a flood, the Spirit of the Lord shall lift up a standard against him.' Prince Grace's time has come to be king. Many of you feel that he is too young, but I believe he will make an excellent king. Don't let his age fool you. A lion's cub seems like no threat, but once he grows up, he becomes the king of beasts. Grace needs your support as a people in these rough times. Serpentine wants us to bow to his power, but we will not. Serpentine will not win because we have God on our side."

He turned to face the young prince who was seated next to him. "Arise, Prince Grace." Schracton placed the royal crown on Grace's head. "May God bless you, King Grace. I pray that His Spirit will be upon you and give wisdom in the difficult times which lie ahead."

Once again he faced the crowd, "Join with me – Long live the king!"

Everyone shouted in unison, "Long live the king!" with enthusiasm and renewed confidence.

The coronation was awesome. I had never seen anything like it. I thoroughly enjoyed the celebration, but once it was over, I walked away to write in my journal.

"Well, things are looking up for our

people. We now have a new king. I believe

King Grace will be an excellent leader. His

father was a great man. He allowed me to be

released from prison. Schracton gave a great

speech. Nolan is walking my way, so I must

go.

Olof, the Great"

"What were you writing?" Nolan asked.

"I was writing in my journal about what happened today."

"Olof, I want to talk to you for a moment."

"What about?"

"After seeing your fighting skills, I want you to help me train the others how to fight. Everyone must become a soldier for us to win this battle. King Grace wants everyone trained to fight with swords as well as bows and arrows. We also have crossbows. Everyone in every village must be trained, from children to adults."

"You want me to help you train the people?"

"That's right. I already spoke to King Grace about you. I will also be teaching you a few things as well. We learned a lot of new techniques since you were in the army."

"I'm willing to learn."

"Good! We'll start early in the morning in the Frilch village. We'd better get going. We have a busy day ahead of us." Nolan put his arm around my shoulder as we walked off to join the others.

* * * * *

"So King, what did you think about the letter my master wrote to you?" Lexon asked with a smirk on his face.

"Well, I've had sometime to think about it," King Grace replied.

"What is your decision, little boy?"

"I have decided not to give you the last Xenonites."

"You fool! You will let your sweet mother die for one hundred ungrateful people who think you are too young to be king? That's crazy!"

"No, it's not! You know that the prophecies will be fulfilled through those people."

"Do you really believe those prophecies? Schracton made that up. If you refuse, then I have no other choice but to destroy your little kingdom and kill everyone, including you."

"Bring it on, Lexon. Tell Serpentine that in the end we will be the victors."

"Sure you will. I will kill you myself and take over this castle. But there really doesn't have to be a fight if you will just surrender the Xenonites to me now. You could have peace the rest of your days… you and your mother."

"My answer remains the same, Lexon!"

Lexon stood up, knocking his chair to the floor. As he strode away, King Grace said, "Tell my mother that I love her."

"Sure, I'll tell her right before she dies."

King Grace watched as Lexon walked away. Tears fell from his eyes.

* * * * *

Early the next morning Nolan began training the Frilch villagers in warfare. From sun up to sun down, breaking only for meals, they practiced two-handed sword swinging and sparring. Nolan demonstrated fighting moves with me. He was a lot younger and quicker than I was, but I overwhelmed him with my strength. He showed me a lot of tactics that I hadn't seen before. It was exhilarating and exhausting.

After sundown, we were ready for bed. I sat talking with Garl. "How long have you been married, Garl?"

"Only two years. I hope to see three."

"Why do you say that?"

"Because of the war. You know a lot of us are going to die."

"Don't be so negative, Garl. You'll make it."

Garl grabbed me by my shirt. "You need to stop living in a fantasy world. You see what has been happening! We're getting killed left and right! The Dark Wolves are winning!"

"Things are going to change because now all of the villagers will be trained as warriors."

"So what? You just don't get it, Olof. Who can defeat Serpentine?"

"We can, if we all work together. Garl, you shouldn't give up so fast."

"Don't tell me that," he demanded. "I lost my whole family in this war, including my first wife!"

I was stunned; I didn't know what to say. Now it made sense why he was so negative. He'd been through a lot.

"Hey, Garl, I'm sorry to hear that. But I know it's going to get better."

"You can't say anything unless you've walked a mile in my shoes."

Garl got up and walked off to his tent. I remained by the fire reading the "Poems of the Lion" until I fell asleep.

* * * * *

When I woke up the next morning, I went over to a nearby tree to practice with my sword. Sweat was pouring down my face as I swung at the tree with all my might. Everyone else was still asleep, including Nolan. After I finished, I sat on a rock and prayed for my father's recovery. Nolan walked up to me and put his hand on my shoulder.

"Sorry to interrupt you, Olof, but it looks like we might have some problems. I got a message from the king stating that an attack is imminent."

"Why is that?"

"Well, the king met with Lexon yesterday morning. Lexon offered him a deal -- that Queen Selena, the king's mother, would be spared if King Grace would deliver the remaining Xenonites to him. King Grace refused and now the Dark Wolves are preparing for battle."

"You mean King Grace risked the life of his mother for his people?"

"Yes, he did. King Grace cares for his people, just as his father did. I consider it an honor to serve as one of his royal guards."

"Well, I guess we must be prepared at all times."

"That's true, Olof. Keep practicing. I must wake the others."

* * * * *

"So, Lexon, are you saying the king prefers war instead of peace?"

"Yes, Master," Lexon replied.

"This war is destined to happen. Gather all troops for battle. We shall utterly destroy the land of Farlon. Why waste any more time, we shall crush them all! The seed of the serpent shall crush the seed of the woman!"

"So what is our plan, Master?" Waldor inquired. "Well, since we don't know where the rest of the Xenonites are, then we must crush all tribes! Start the attack at once!"

Nearby, in the Frilch village, Olaf sat writing in his journal.

"I have been totally encouraged
lately. I feel at peace. Regardless of
everything that has happened, I feel as if I
am walking on clouds. I am at peace with
God. I am second in command with training
the troops. My father is getting better
everyday. I hear he is now eating and
walking a little bit, that he almost has full

strength in both of his legs. It seems as if

Garl has given up hope, but I think he's

going to make it. I see a messenger coming

towards me, so I must go.

Olof, the Great"

"Hello, my name is Lark. I have a very important

message that must be relayed to the royal guard Nolan."

"You can tell me and I will tell Nolan. I'm second

in command."

"The village of Harlon is under attack! Our soldiers

can't hold them off much longer," Lark said in a fretful

voice.

"Orion is there!"

"What did you say?"

"Never mind. I must tell Nolan." I immediately ran

to wake Nolan and tell him the news.

"What is it, Olof?"

"The village of Harlon is under attack, I must get there quickly!"

"Olof, we must remain here. It's too dangerous! You must stay here. Those are my orders!"

"I cannot follow your orders when my sister is in danger!"

"All right then, wake the others. We will go there together, but if any life is lost, it is your responsibility. You made the decision."

"I accept it. I just hope my sister is alright."

* * * * *

We mounted our horses and headed to the village Harlon. The fighting was fierce. I didn't see who was leading the attack. Our troops arrived just in time and fought off the remaining Dark Wolves. Karas was wounded, suffering a bad cut to his arm. Luckily, the Dark Wolves never made it inside the village. All the villagers had fled through the tunnels. I was really hoping to see my little sister as we searched for survivors.

Nolan looked at me. "Well, Olof, you have led us to our first battle and we were successful. I'm proud of you."

"Thanks, Nolan."

"Everyone, we're going to rest here for the night. In the morning we will practice our battle exercises and begin training the Harlan people."

I looked over at Makka. She seemed very sad, so I went over to talk with her.

"What's the matter?"

"Nothing much."

"Well, you look pretty bothered. Are you sure?"

"I was just thinking about my husband."

"He died?"

"Yes, he did. He sacrificed his life protecting me, so I could make it to the tunnel."

"That was pretty heroic."

"Yes, but now I'm alone."

"That's not true. You still have your father and we are all your family." I smiled at her, hoping to cheer her up.

"That's nice to hear. I'm sorry for avoiding you, Olof, not speaking to you when you told us you were a criminal."

"It's okay, I don't blame you. I probably would have done the same thing."

"My father says you're going to make a great leader."

"That's pretty nice of him to say that. What do you think?"

"I think you're old," Makka said as she burst out laughing.

"Very funny, very funny. I'm only thirty-six.

"Why, you're almost as old as my father."

"It's past your bedtime, young lady. Go get some sleep."

I couldn't sleep. I stayed up reading *The Poems of the Lion.* I heard a noise in the bushes. I grabbed the Sword of Judah and went to investigate.

"Don't kill me! I'm a Xenonite," a fearful voice said.

When I got closer, I saw it was my brother Syphon. Both of his arms had been burned and he looked very weak. I embraced him and started to cry.

"I'm so sorry, Syphon. I'm sorry for what I did. I'm sorry about Momma... I'm so sorry."

"It's okay, Olof. Really, it's alright."

I woke everyone up to introduce my brother. Tira bandaged his arms and had him lie down on her bed to rest.

Glotus and Ari walked up to me. "Is that your older brother?" Ari asked.

"Yes, one of them. His name is Syphon."

"You thought he was dead?" Glotus asked.

"I sure did. I didn't think any of my family made it out alive."

"Well, God surprised you. One of them is still alive," Ari remarked with excitement in his voice.

"I'm so grateful Syphon is alive because I never got to tell him I'm sorry."

"About what?" Ari asked curiously.

"We had a lot of disagreements. We never got along. We always fought each other."

"Now it's time for reconciliation," Glotus said.

"True! I can't wait until he gets better so we can talk more."

Glotus and Ari headed back to bed and I wrote in my journal.

> "God, you are so awesome. I thought
> that Syphon had not survived the attack, but
> somehow you spared him. I can't wait to
> talk with him more. Your word is true -- all

things work together for the good of those
that love you. You are a blessing to my life.
I thank you, God.

Olof,

the Great"

"So how has the battle been going?" King Grace
was concerned.

"There was only one small invasion in the village of
Harlon," Nile reported.

"Were there many deaths?"

"Only about ten on our side, Your Highness. The
enemy suffered a greater loss," Lages bragged.

"That was only a diversion. They are planning a
larger attack. Everyone needs to be on guard. Make sure the

castle is secured, as well as all of the villages. How is the training of the villagers coming along?"

Colan answered, "Everything is going very well, Sire. We have reports from all of the villages that a mighty army is arising."

"That's very good," the king replied with a smile.

Daqual spoke up. "We have some bad news though, King Grace."

"What is it, Daqual?"

"The prophet Schracton is deathly ill. Reports say that he is not doing well."

"Prepare a horse for me right away. I must see him," the king commanded.

* * * * *

"Nolan, how are we doing with our training?" Balsk inquired.

"Everyone is doing fine, but the real test is on the battlefield," Nolan replied.

"When is that going to be?" Hoi wondered.

"It will be very soon. We are going to be fighting on their ground next. Our plan is to fight all the way to Varcraine Castle and destroy it," said Nolan.

"Are you serious? That castle is highly guarded. There's no way we can take it down, Nolan," Garl spoke up in a doubtful tone.

"Garl, you seem to forget. God is on our side. We can do it," I said in an optimistic tone.

"Yes, at the risk of all of our lives," Garl shouted, then turned and walked away. Tira ran over to Garl to calm him down.

"How soon do we attack?" I asked.

"Very soon, Olof. When the king gets back from his visit with Schracton, all of the royal guards will meet with him to plan the attack," Nolan replied.

"How is Schracton faring?" Makka asked.

"Not too good. They believe that he is going to die soon."

"If we don't have a prophet, how are we to win the war?" Celon sounded worried.

"Don't lose heart, Celon. God is with us. There will always be a prophet among us," Balsk said.

"We have plenty of soldiers who are busy making swords and arrows as we speak," Nolan said.

Pereal spoke up. "I'm going with you."

"Father, you can't go. You're too old and besides that, you're just now getting better." I was astonished that he would even suggest such a thing.

"Son, I'm going. I must repay Lexon for the bruise on my head," he said with authority, leaning on his staff.

"Let's get some rest tonight. We have a lot more training to do in the morning," Nolan said.

* * * * *

"How are you feeling, Schracton?"

"Not too good, my king. I'm pretty weak," Schracton said between coughs.

"You have to get better. You must prepare us for battle with your prayers to God."

"I'm sorry, my king, but I won't be the one to lead the people into battle with prayer. God will raise up another prophet."

"Not so, Schracton, you can make it," said Grace, trying to hold back his tears.

"It's okay to cry, young Grace. You must release your emotions. It's not good to keep them bottled up inside. I shall anoint another prophet tomorrow and before the sun goes down, I will die and go to be with God in Heaven."

"No! Don't say that. It can't be true," King Grace sobbed.

"I'm sorry, young Grace, but it is true. I know that you have seen a lot of death for one so young, but death is a part of life. Remember this, Grace, God shall comfort you in these times."

"Why do you have to die now when I need you most?" asked Grace, his desperation increasing.

"God has called me home, but we will meet again," Schracton said, gripping the king's hand tightly.

Weary after their long talk, Schracton fell asleep. King Grace emerged from the cave to announce the anointing of a new prophet.

* * * * *

The next day everyone gathered in Schracton's village of Barras. Two of the royal guards, Daqual and Nile, helped to assist Schracton to stand before the waiting crowd.

"I have been the prophet in the land of Farlon for four hundred years. It is time for me to be with God, so when the sun goes down tonight, I will pass on. But, before

96

I do, I am charged by God to anoint the next prophet. This man is from the tribe Biscal. God showed this man to me in a vision. God will use him to take our people farther than I did, but in less time than I did in my four hundred years. I ask that you come forward, young Swalo."

Swalo rose from where he was sitting among the people and walked to stand next to Schracton. Swalo was about five feet tall, weighing one hundred five pounds, and only eighteen years of age. Schracton put his hand over Swalo's head and prayed over him.

"God, I pray for Swalo that Your hand will be upon him from this day forward. Fill this young man with wisdom. Guide him with Your righteous right hand and keep him in Your loving arms. Let him walk among Your people. We beseech you to allow Your signs and wonders to manifest through him."

Many people were shocked because Swalo was so young. A man standing next to me cried out, "Why, he is just a baby, still in diapers and in need of his mommy!"

After he said it, before he could laugh, he fell down dead.

* * * * *

Just after sunset, Schracton passed away. I wrote in my journal.

"I can't believe that Schracton has died. Having heard so much about him, then finally getting to meet him, it now seems such a short a time that I have known him. Swalo will be an excellent prophet. I know God's hand is upon him. Now we unite as a people to fight the most deadly battle ever, to take down the Varcraine Castle. Only God can get us through this one.

Olof, the Great"

"This meeting will be brief. We have a war that is escalating like never before. I believe our best strategy is to invade the Varcraine Castle."

"What are your plans Sire?" Colan asked.

"Daqual, Nile, Colan, Lages, and one thousand of our best soldiers shall remain at the castle with me, unless plans change. You other five guards will take your troops up five different paths leading to Varcraine Castle. Take no prisoners. The enemy must be crushed. Swalo will accompany Nolan's group up the most difficult path through the Solo Mountains. Are there any questions?" the king asked.

"Why does the prophet go into battle with us now? It wasn't like this before," Daqual asked.

Swalo replied, "Daqual, God is doing a new thing."

Nobody else spoke as they all left the room.

* * * * *

We sat around at the Harlon village eating and having fun. Pereal was telling stories about things that happened when he was a youth. I never knew my father was such a great storyteller. We all grabbed our swords when we heard noises, and then saw people coming out of the tunnels. I couldn't believe my eyes, it was Orion and her family. I ran and hugged her as tight as I could.

"Olof, I can't breathe," she said, so I finally let her go.

"I'm so glad to see you!" My enthusiasm was obvious.

"I can tell, Olof. Let me introduce you to my family. This is my husband Quayle, my daughter Lola, and my two sons, Worle and Charf."

"Wow, look at you! You have grown up and have a family of your own. Orion, you look just like Momma."

"Thanks, Olof. What a nice thing to say."

I noticed one last person coming from the tunnels. It was Phlax.

He picked me up in a big bear hug. "Little brother, I thought I'd never see you again. I thought you and Father and Syphon all died together. I barely escaped after I saw Syphon die."

"What do you mean? Syphon is still alive. They're nursing him back to health as we speak," I said.

"No way, Olof. I saw them kill him. I was right there." I grabbed Phlax by the hand and took him to the tent where Syphon was staying. Syphon was standing at the entrance. He walked up to me, smiled, and then punched me in the face, knocking me to the ground.

"Syphon, why did you hit me?" I said, rubbing my sore chin.

"Maybe because I am not Syphon. I'm Malgrim," he said.

I watched as the man I thought was Syphon turned into the hideous Malgrim. He gave a loud whistle and immediately Mulcham and other underground warriors burst out of the ground like unwanted weeds. They were horrible looking -- dark green bodies, the top half looked like men except for the foot-long claws on their hands. These monsters had tongues and fangs like snakes and from the waist down instead of legs they had long, wide tails, which they used to burrow through the dirt. Mulcham and his twenty warriors engaged our troops while I fought Malgrim. He punched me twice and kicked me in the throat. I fell to the ground, clinching my neck and gasping for air. I prayed to God for strength, then grabbed Malgrim and threw him into a tree.

"Just give me the Sword of Judah and we will leave peacefully," Malgrim said.

I pulled out the sword and charged at him. He drew his sword and we clashed. The Sword of Judah glowed and cut his sword in two. I swung again, barely missing him. He grabbed me by the arm and threw me to the ground. The sword fell out of my hand. As I went to grab it, he kicked me in the face. When he tried to kick me again, I looked at him and saw him thrown into a tree. I thought to myself, *how did I do that?*

Fighting him was hard because my hand was still broken. He ran towards me and I tackled him to the ground. He lifted me up by my neck and held me suspended in the air. His look was pure evil. "I killed your brother Syphon and now I'm going to kill you!"

Tears fell from my eyes as I looked for the Sword of Judah. Although it was out of reach, I yelled, "NOW!"

The sword flew from the ground into Malgrim's back. He disappeared and I fell to the ground. Mulcham saw this and said in fear, "Soldiers, we must retreat!"

All of the underground warriors fled quickly. I just sat there on my knees, crying, unable to stop. No one could begin to comfort me because of the pain I felt in my heart. The enemy had played on my emotions and nearly defeated us. I learned a horrible lesson that night: Something that looks good can still be evil.

Phlax ran to embrace me. "You killed Malgrim! Olof, you saved all of us! This is not a time for sorrow; it's a time for rejoicing. Get up and rejoice! God gave us victory!"

Phlax helped me to my feet as the others hugged me and cheered for me. I really felt like a winner. That night we threw a big celebration. Nolan, Swalo, and another one thousand soldiers walked into the camp wondering what all the partying was about.

Nolan walked up to Balsk. "Why the celebration, Balsk?"

"Well, Nolan, there's nothing but good news. Olof defeated Malgrim while you were gone. That young man is a great asset to this army. He is definitely a man of honor and courage."

"Indeed he is. Is everyone else okay?"

"No lives were lost, just bruises and other minor injuries."

"Great! That's good to hear. Well, let's enjoy the party. I'll meet with everyone tomorrow morning."

* * * * *

Later, I sat near some bushes talking with my father. "So, son, I can see your life has really changed for the better. Did all of this come about while you were in prison?"

"No, Father. I was very frustrated and confused while I was locked up. I had a lot of time to think, though. I read two good books and wrote in my journal. But my real change came when I got out and talked with the prophet Schracton. He really made me think about my life without God. I saw myself as totally without anything and God wanted to heal my broken heart. I repented my sins and accepted Jesus as my Lord and Savior. The stories in this book that Schracton wrote really began to touch me. Knowing that God became man, dwelt in the land of

Farlon, and died on a cross for my sins has taken on new meaning for me."

"That's good. I'm glad you found something to make your life better."

"Father, God can do the same thing in your life, if you'll let him."

"I'm okay, Olof. I don't need God. I've been doing great without him."

"Well, just know that if you ever need Him, he's only a prayer away."

"Okay, now let's go enjoy the party."

* * * * *

Phlax and two young boys walked up to me. "Olof, this is my son Nigel, and this is Syphon's boy, Greg," he said, introducing me.

"How old are you?" I asked.

Nigel said, "We're both twelve."

Greg said, "What was it like in prison, Olof?"

"It was horrible. I hated every day of it," I told him.

"It's rude to ask him about that," scolded Phlax.

"Where are your mothers?" I asked.

"Neither one of them survived the invasion," Phlax replied in a somber tone.

I was shocked at how much Greg looked like Syphon. He was the spitting image of him. They both had a dark spot on the left side of their face.

"Come on, Greg, let's go eat," said Nigel. Both of them ran off together.

"You have to pray for Greg," said Phlax. "He's taking it pretty hard."

"Yes, I see it all over his face. It's going to get better for him in time, though," I said.

"Hopefully sooner than later, Olof. He's been a troublemaker since birth. Losing his parents just adds to the flames."

"So, who's going to raise him?"

"I am. Father is getting too old to be raising kids again."

"I guess I'd better get some rest, Phlax. I'll see you in the morning."

I walked to my tent, sat down, and pulled out my journal.

"Well a lot has changed. Phlax and Syphon have children. My little sister Orion has three of her own. We're engaged in a horrible war with the Dark Wolves. There's no way to escape. All of the men, women, and children have to become warriors. I'm glad that not too many have died, but I know there will be casualties. The book that Schracton gave me has really taught me a lot. Well, I'd better get some rest.

Olof, the

Great"

* * * * *

The next morning Orion's daughter Lola awakened me. Nolan had called for a meeting with the whole camp. He stood up and began speaking.

"My brothers and sisters, the other day I had a meeting with King Grace. We are going to invade Serpentine's castle. Our group will be taking the route that leads through the Solo Mountains. This is going to be a treacherous journey. The king is sending more soldiers, so there will be a total of fifty thousand troops. We also have a dove to send and receive messages from the king. As soon as the other soldiers arrive, we will begin our journey. The goal of this group is to take Serpentine by surprise. They will not be expecting us to go through the mountains. I need everyone to gather as much food as possible and we will leave at once."

When Nolan was finished, Swalo walked up to me.

"Olof, hold out your left hand. God is going to heal you."

I held out my hand. Swalo touched it and instantly I was totally healed. The troops that the king sent walked into the camp afterwards.

Nolan walked up to Swalo and asked, "How many people do we have total?"

"Fifty-one thousand, two hundred fifty-one people altogether."

* * * * *

We began our journey, walking the Swiss trail. This trail had no grass, but plenty of rocks of all sizes. Most of us were on horses. The women and children rode inside carriages, which also held food and other provisions.

Nolan rode beside me. "Olof, I need you to send letters to the king for me. Whatever I tell you, write it down, then attach the letter to the leg of this dove. It will fly straight to the king with the message. I believe we will eventually need more soldiers. This is going to be some very tough fighting."

"Nolan, it's going to be alright," I said confidently.

* * * * *

"Well, looks like the score is two to one. We took care of the king and queen and they got Malgrim. My sources tell me there are five groups of soldiers coming to take our kingdom, but we have plans for them. Waldor, can you send them a welcome party?" Serpentine asked.

"Your wish is my command, Master," Waldor replied.

"We will crush them, one group at a time. You may leave my presence," Serpentine said with a smile.

All of the generals left the room leaving the grinning madman alone.

* * * * *

"Sire, we have just received a report from the battle," Nile said.

"Read it to me," King Grace said with authority.

"Dear King Grace,

This is Lotus, one of your royal guards. While traveling up the trail, invading troops caught us by surprise. We lost fifty-two soldiers in the battle. However, regardless of the difficulties, we are still going forward. Long live the king!

Lotus"

"This is not good. It's as if they knew we were coming," said the king.

"How can that be?" Daqual asked.

"Because there is a traitor among us. Nile, Colan, Lages, grab Daqual."

The three of them wrestled Daqual down to the ground.

"God showed me that you had betrayed us, Daqual, but it doesn't matter. We will continue our same battle plan. Take him and lock him in the dungeon." The king was furious.

"Do you want us to send more troops to help Lotus?" Lages asked.

"Actually, what I want you to do is this. Send out three more groups that have ten thousand men apiece. I want you three to each lead a group. We are going to surprise Serpentine and his army like never before," the king replied.

"But what about you, Sire?" asked Colan.

"I will be alright. I'm in God's hands. He will protect me," the king replied.

The three guards took Daqual and put him in the dungeon.

* * * * *

The next day as our troops moved up the Swiss trail, it started to rain. Soon we were soaking wet. I noticed Greg sitting in the carriage, so I rode up next to him to keep him company.

"So Greg, how do you like the rain?" I asked.

"I don't. You know my father didn't like you and guess what, I don't either!"

"Why is that, Greg? Why don't you like me?"

"I just don't! So go talk to someone else who wants to listen to you."

"Okay, if that's what you want," I said. I rode off to catch up with Nolan.

* * * * *

"Nolan, we're under attack!" Rinu yelled.

"It's an air attack," screamed Makka.

I looked up to see Vulcore, a woman with feathers all over her body, large wings, and legs like a bird. She let out a cry and hundreds of large black ravens followed her

114

carrying large stones in their talons. They flew down on us dropping rocks. It seemed like it was raining boulders. One rock hit one of the carriages and broke off a wheel. Another rock hit the horses' harnesses of the same carriage. I watched as the horses ran off in a panic.

Nolan looked ahead. " There are some wolves coming after us as well. Troops get out front and try to fight them off!"

Glotus got hit with a boulder. He and his horse were lying down on the ground, not moving at all. Vine pulled him up onto his own horse.

"Swalo, how many soldiers have we lost?" asked Nolan.

Swalo replied, "We have already lost three hundred fifteen men."

The wolves viciously attacked us, jumping up to sink their teeth into them and yanking the men off their horses.

"Hurry! We must make it to the caves," Nolan shouted. "That's our only hope!"

Ari fought off a few wolves as he swung his sword. I saw Waldor, the evil henchman that talked to animals near the caves. He must have sent the wolves. A rock had wounded my horse, so I had to dismount and run to hitch a ride in a carriage.

I watched as one by one our soldiers were crushed by boulders, and then eaten by ravenous wolves. As we headed towards the caves, I saw Lexon and about one hundred warriors come out. I was horseless. There was nothing I could do. Suddenly, a thought came to mind, *I'll write a quick note to the king.*

"Your Highness, King Grace,

My name is Olof, one of your trusted servants. I am in Nolan's group. We are in a fierce battle. We need more troops. We have lost three hundred fifteen men. We are under attack from three different angles. Please send help soon. God help us.

Olof, the

Great"

I quickly tied the note to the dove and cast him upward into the sky. " Fly to the king, little bird!" The dove flew off to the royal castle.

Lexon and his soldiers came at us full force slaughtering our soldiers. No one was able to stand up against him. Large rocks hit some of the soldiers that had tried to flee. Finally, Nolan met up with Lexon. Their fight seemed to go on for hours as I watched helplessly from the carriage.

Finally, I grabbed my bow and arrow to try to take Lexon down. I aimed at his head, then let the arrow fly. Lexon caught the arrow in his hand and looked over at me. "So, little boy, you want to shoot me?" The arrow in his hand burst into flame as he put it in his bow and shot it back at me. The arrow flew inside the carriage, igniting the interior, but luckily, everyone made it out alive.

Then our most deadly battle began on Death Bridge, a large stone bridge above the Algin River, which was home to hundreds of alligators. It was called "Death Bridge" because if you fell off, the alligators ensured that you wouldn't live to tell anyone about it. Nonetheless, I grabbed the Sword of Judah and began to fight. Our soldiers knocked down the giant ravens and Vulcore retreated. We knew if we could just stop the wolves, we might survive. I think God heard my prayers. Swalo pointed his staff at Waldor and a surge of power came from it and hit Waldor, knocking him to the ground. The wolves immediately retreated. Our remaining troops fought off Lexon and his warriors, and they fled as well.

We finally made it to the caves. I looked around to see who hadn't made it. Glotus, Hoi, and Joles were the ones from our original group who were killed, but there were also many others. Swalo came forward to speak.

"Men, women, and children… we started off with fifty-one thousand, two hundred fifty-one people in this group. Now we only have fifty thousand and this was our first battle. We are not even at the Solo Mountains. We must be encouraged and not lose heart. God says that we are more than conquerors. One day we shall make it to the Varcraine Castle and crush Serpentine. The time is coming soon."

I looked at Greg who was sitting all by himself. He seemed frightened from the battle. I went over and hugged him. "Greg, everything is going to be okay."

"How do you know? We're all going to die! Don't you get it? We can't win. Serpentine has always beaten us. They killed my father and they're going to kill all of us." His frustration was apparent, and then he started crying.

I held him even tighter. "God will protect us. It will be alright."

Greg pulled away from me with an angry look on his face. "God isn't here with us. He's not real. He wasn't there when my mother and father got killed. Now leave me alone!" He got up and stormed away.

Makka came over to talk to me. "Just give him time. He'll see the light someday."

"I don't know, Makka. He seems just like his father... stubborn, with a deadly temper."

"Trust me, Olof, he'll be okay."

"So how are you feeling about this war?"

"Not good at first, but I know it's going to get better."

"But when, Makka? I just want to know when."

"With God on our side, Olof, we can't lose."

"Yes, that's true and one day God is going to save Greg."

"That's the spirit, Olof! Don't let the enemy take the victory from you."

"Thanks a lot, Makka. One day you will make someone a great wife."

"Trust me, Olof, I'm not getting married again. I lost my husband when our village was raided. I'm not getting married again so I won't go through that heartache a second time."

"Yes, I hear what you're saying. That must have been pretty tough."

"It was. Now I have to get back and tend to my father. He was wounded in the fight. See you, Olof. We'll talk later."

* * * * *

"Sire, we just got reports back from the troops," Narx said excitedly.

"So what has happened?" King Grace asked.

"Shaw and his troops are doing fine. They haven't met any opposition. Nolan lost three hundred fifteen in a horrible battle. Lotus's camp was invaded at midnight and they lost three thousand people. War is doing very well. They faced two battles, wiped out a thousand enemy soldiers and lost only one hundred men. Regal is in grave danger. Their forces are being destroyed and Regal was wounded in the chest by an arrow."

"We need to send reinforcements for Regal, at least another ten thousand soldiers. Has there been any news of the enemy trying to invade the castle?"

"Not yet, Sire. We haven't heard of any planned invasions on the castle. How are you faring, my Lord?"

"Not too good. I've had a lot of sleepless nights since I became king. Now I am more nervous than ever concerning the outcome."

"My king, you carry the heavy burden of the kingdom on your shoulders."

"You're right, Narx. Sometimes I feel I'm too young to be on the throne."

"That's not the case, Sire. You have the wisdom of your father. He was a great man. You remind me of him. Just get some rest, my Lord. We have everything else under control."

Narx left the room, leaving the king sitting there, thinking about what he'd said.

* * * * *

The next morning Garl kicked me in the leg to awaken me.

"It's time to get up, old man!"

"Excuse me, but you're about as old as I am."

"Not even close, Olof. You look like you're eighty," Garl said with a smile.

"We'll see when this old man knocks you on the ground."

We started wrestling, and then Nolan broke it up. "Hey, quit clowning around. Hurry up and grab some food before I beat both of you up."

"Oh sure, you and what army?" Garl asked before he ran off to get something to eat.

As Nolan helped me up, I smelled the fresh baked bread and scrambled eggs mixed with onions that were almost done. I ran over to get some food. Tira handed me a plate with plenty of bread and eggs on it. I sat down next to Celon to eat.

"That's a pretty big plate, Olaf. If you can't eat it all, pass it to me."

"Trust me, I can eat every bite of it," I said, guarding my plate.

"I can't wait until we get to Varcraine Castle so I can personally repay Serpentine."

"Well, if I remember correctly, Celon, you were running from Lexon the other night."

"Not even! I stood up to him, but my horse ran in the other direction." We both laughed, and then quickly gobbled our food down so we could catch up with the others.

* * * * *

The room was pitch black. They could barely see each other. Everyone waited patiently until they finally heard the footsteps of their long-awaited leader. They looked out of the corner of their eyes to make sure it was him. The two-headed figure was enraged.

"What happened the other night, Lexon?" Serpentine demanded to know.

"Master, what do you mean? We killed over a thousand of their soldiers."

"So that is supposed to impress me? Where is the Sword of Judah? The owner is supposed to be dead and the Xenonites are still alive!"

A serpent burst forth out of the ground. The other generals fled into each corner of the room like frightened children. The serpent wrapped itself around Lexon's leg like a rope.

"Tell me, Lexon, why I shouldn't kill you right now," Serpentine demanded.

Lexon voice trembled. "Because I'm a benefit to your army, Master."

"How are you a benefit? You can't even do a simple task like retrieve a sword for me. You have been demoted. Tarlenum is going to replace you and take care of the Xenonites."

The serpent let go of Lexon and disappeared. Lexon got up off the floor grateful for his life.

"Tarlenum, come forward," Serpentine ordered. The huge, one-eyed ogre approached his master, ready for battle.

"Are you ready for your task?" Serpentine asked.

"Yes sir," the ogre spoke with boldness.

"I want you to bring me the Sword of Judah, kill all the Xenonites, and bring me the head of Olof."

"Who is Olof, Master?"

"He is the temporary owner of the Sword of Judah."

"No problem, sir. It shall be done as you commanded."

Without another word, Serpentine strode out of the dark room, leaving his generals alone.

* * * * *

As we traveled through the caves, Nigel and Phlax came over to me.

"Uncle Olof, can I see your sword?"

"Of course, Nigel. Here you go. Just be careful."

Nigel could barely hold the sword because of its weight. He swung it like a golf club at the rocks on the ground.

"Tell me, Phlax. How far are we from the castle?"

"At least one month's journey, if not more, Olof. We still have to reach Solo Mountains."

"I think Nigel is going to be just as strong as you are, if not stronger."

"You think so?"

"Definitely! Look at his size now and he's only twelve. I can't wait to get married someday and have a son like him."

"Slow down, Olof. It will come in good time, little brother. This isn't a good time to be married. Your wife could be here today, then gone tomorrow."

"Phlax, how was your wife?"

"Jessica was very nice. She was always there for me, in good and bad times. You know, I never thought I'd be without her. It seemed like we would be together forever."

"I bet Nigel misses her a lot."

"Yes. He cries himself to sleep every night."

"Here you go, Uncle Olof," Nigel said, handing me my sword.

"Thanks, Nigel," I said, returning the sword to its sheath.

"What's so special about the Sword of Judah?" Nigel asked.

"Well, Nigel, this sword has a lot of power. It's basically as strong as the character of the one who holds it. If that person has a horrible character, then the sword is useless. But if the person has a pure heart, then the Sword of Judah becomes the best weapon in the world."

"Wow! That's amazing, Uncle Olof. Do you know how to use it pretty well?"

"I'm learning, Nigel. I'm still learning."

* * * * *

I grabbed an apple and my journal from my bag and began writing.

"Nigel seems like a good boy. It's Greg that I'm worried about. He always isolates himself from everyone. Well, not everyone, he does play with Nigel. Maybe one day Nigel's good character will rub off on him. I have to keep praying for Greg and hope for the best. Your word is truly a lamp to my feet. I thank you, God, for all you're doing--seen and unseen.

Olof, the Great"

* * * * *

I was awakened that night by a loud commotion. Karas said, "Get up Olof. We're surrounded by ogres."

As I got up I grabbed the Sword of Judah and made ready to fight. One of the ogres punched Dranu and he flew into me, knocking both of us to the ground. The ogres had huge clubs in their hands. We had an advantage because they were very slow.

Nolan yelled, "Run! There are too many of them!"

The caves were like a big maze. There was hardly any room in the caves to put up a fight. We had no choice but to run. After we made it to a large open area, we decided to fight. I cut one of the ogres' clubs in half. He picked me up and threw me into the cave wall. I got up and ran toward him, kicking him in the chest and swinging my sword, but the ogre blocked it. Though I'd kicked him as hard as I could, it didn't seem to bother him one bit. The ogre swung at me, but I quickly moved and kicked him in the eye. I looked to see how many of our men had been defeated. It was one huge graveyard. Not one of the ogres had been stopped. I looked at Nolan. Surrender was written all over him.

Nolan yelled, "Retreat men, retreat! Olof, write a letter to the king, then run!"

"Dear King Grace,

This is Olof from Nolan's army. Ogres are crushing us. Send help immediately.

Olof, the Great"

One of the ogres was about to grab Greg, so I threw the Sword of Judah at him with all my might. The sword hit the ogre in the arm and he disappeared. As I went to grab the sword, a black raven came out of nowhere and beat me to it. It picked up the sword and flew off before I could catch it.

"NOOOO!!" I screamed.

One of the ogres looked at me and said, "It looks like you lost something."

As we fled the area, the slow ogres tried their best to pursue us. They couldn't catch us, but we sustained a horrible loss anyway -- the Sword of Judah was now in enemy hands.

"I can't believe I allowed the sword to be taken."

"It's alright, Olof," said Nolan.

"No, it's not. Now we're definitely going to lose."

"Why do you give up so easily? Is that what you're going to do every time you suffer a loss, just call it quits? Well, since you're a big quitter, why don't you just turn around and go back to Pasqual village, Olof?"

"What did you say?" I asked, becoming angry.

"You heard me, go home. We don't need any crybabies around here."

My anger overcame me. I tackled Nolan, ramming him into a wall of dirt. He got up and kicked me twice in the leg. I felt so much pain that I fell to the ground. Nolan jumped on top of me, pummeling my face until I was unable to move.

Phlax was furious and rushed to stop Nolan, but Swalo stopped him. "This is Olof's fight. Let them be."

As I got up off the ground, I took a swing at Nolan. He moved out of my way, and then kicked me in my back. "Your temper makes you a horrible fighter. Come on, quitter, I've got some more for you."

Nolan grabbed me, picked me up, and then threw me to the ground. "Go ahead and quit, Olof. This is what you're known for, isn't it? Olof, the quitter." Nolan grabbed my leg and twisted it. "Are you going to quit now?"

"No!"

He twisted harder. "What about now?"

"No!"

He twisted it again even harder. I felt as if my leg was going to break in two.

"Go ahead, quitter. Call it quits, you baby!"

"Never!"

This time when he twisted, I was sure that would be the end of my leg. I burst out crying and Nolan let go of my leg. He knelt next to me and whispered in my ear. "We had to get that quitter mentality out of your system before it kills you. Don't let your temper do the same."

As I lay there on the ground crying, everyone else walked away.

* * * * *

"Well, it seems that victory is ours. Let me show you why. Tarlenum, show these men what you received the other day."

Tarlenum held up the Sword of Judah. "Truly, victory is ours."

"Not only did Tarlenum and his ogres get the Sword of Judah, they also destroyed over five thousand enemy soldiers. I'm sending him back out to finish the job, but they need some allies with speed. That's why Mulcham and his underground warriors will be working with you. The plan is to destroy the whole army that is trying to invade us through the Solo Mountains."

When Serpentine finished his speech he disappeared.

* * * * *

"This is terrible news," said King Grace.

"I know, Your Highness," replied Narx.

"We're going to take a chance, Narx. Send out another twenty thousand troops. The Solo Mountains is the quickest, but most dangerous route to Varcraine Castle."

"But what if Nolan's group is outnumbered?"

"We will have to take that chance. If we don't move now, Nolan's forces will be destroyed. The ogres have no remorse. They kill women and children, the elderly, the sick and wounded as well. Have them take along a few carriages full of extra weapons."

"Yes, Sire. I will do it immediately."

* * * * *

The next day I sat in prayer for two hours. I had a lot to think about--the battle that had taken place and the fight I'd had with Nolan. I learned two things: Bad tempers and quitting will take the strongest of men down. God used Nolan to teach me that. My body was still aching from the beating he gave me. Now I see that you're constantly learning in life.

Olof, the Great"

As I put my pen down, my father walked up to me.

"Olof, don't be too hard on yourself. We haven't lost yet. Trust me, we'll get the sword back."

"I hope so."

"Are you going to get something to eat, Son?"

"Probably later."

"You know, if you don't hurry, Phlax is going to eat it all."

"That's one thing that hasn't changed -- Phlax eating all the food." We both laughed a little at that.

"Are you still in pain, Olof?"

"Yes, a lot of pain."

"You know, Son, I haven't seen anyone beat you up since Roland taught you how to fight."

"Well, Nolan is a good fighter... one of the royal guards."

"You know, Olof, the best man isn't always the toughest man."

"Thanks for saying that."

"Let's get going, Olof. We have a long journey ahead of us."

* * * * *

About a week later, I woke up to shouting in the camp. Our reinforcements had arrived. We just gained twenty thousand more soldiers and five carriages full of weapons. There were daggers, swords, crossbows, and axes. As I sat there looking at the weapons, I couldn't believe my eyes. It was Tiris, Borak, and Ryan. I ran and hugged Tiris.

"I thought you were dead!"

"I thought you were as well, Olof," Tiris replied. "But it would take more than an invasion to kill me."

"Well, that's good to hear. I've been reading the book you gave me. It's taught me a lot. Where is Susan?"

"She's right over there, saying hello to her friends."

"It's so good to see you, Tiris," I hugged him again as tears of joy fell from my eyes.

"Yes, we made it out, but a lot of our family and friends died."

"I know what you mean. My brother Syphon died in the attack. I don't know if you heard, but Schracton gave me the Sword of Judah, but the enemy took it from me in the last battle."

"Things happen, Olof. No need to be disappointed, at least you're alive."

"What happened about you becoming a royal guard?"

"Well, I haven't heard anything from the king yet."

"You would be perfect for the job."

"Thanks, Olof. Do you still have the journal I gave you?"

"Yes, I do. I write in it at least once a week. Look!" I flipped open my journal and showed him every page.

Nolan calmed down the crowd so he could speak to us. "My people, the war is truly on. The king has sent us the help we need. We're getting closer to the Solo Mountains. We have our work cut out for us. The enemy is all around us, but victory is just around the bend. After we eat, we must begin our journey. Long live King Grace! Olof, will you write to the king and let him know we received the help he sent?"

"Yes sir!" I quickly wrote the letter and sent it off with the dove.

"Eat hearty, everyone. You will need a lot of energy for this trip," said Nolan, ending his speech.

* * * * *

"Olof, I'm sorry for the way I acted when we were in the dungeon together."

"It's alright, Ryan. I forgive you."

"You do?"

"Yes, I do. I'm a changed man, Ryan. I'm not that same miserable prisoner you met. I've turned my life over to God."

"Why did you do that?"

"I saw how messed up my life was and knew I needed a change. Have you ever asked God to forgive you of your sins, Ryan?"

"No, I never did. Well, I need to go see if Nolan needs anything." Ryan hurried away. I knew why.

* * * * *

"Swalo, should we continue taking our forces through the caves to the mountains?"

"No, Nolan, they're expecting that. What you should do is send some troops down the Wyle River that flows around the mountains. Those troops would make it to the castle a lot quicker and with less opposition."

"That sounds good. Who should we send?"

"Olof is ready. I think he should lead that group and try to retrieve the sword."

"You really think he's ready?"

"He's ready, Nolan. God will see to it."

"I hope so."

* * * * *

It was raining pretty hard when we awoke the next morning. All the leaves of the trees were wet with Heaven's dew. My garments were soaked and my hair was drenched as if I had bathed in a river. Clouds covered the sun like a blanket over a sleeping child. I grabbed my journal to write.

"All is peaceful right now. Not an enemy in sight, but only for a moment, I'm sure. Peace is sometimes a small benefit of war. Our troops are barely holding on. A lot of them were discouraged by our recent defeat by the ogres. I must get the Sword of Judah back, but I don't think that's going to happen. Serpentine won't give it up without a fight.

Olof, the Great"

Nolan approached me. "How are you doing this morning, Olaf?"

"Pretty good. I didn't sleep much last night."

"Why not?"

"I guess I just wasn't tired."

"Olof let me tell you -- you're going to be an awesome warrior."

"Thanks a lot, Nolan."

"No, I really mean it. I'm sorry about the other day."

"Nolan, you don't need to say that. I owe you an apology. You saw the bad temper and the quitting mentality in my heart and you exposed it. That revelation made me a better man."

"Well, a lot of men wouldn't have received such correction."

"The way I see it, if they realized that it was all true, like I did, they would thank God for it."

"I've been talking to the prophet Swalo and we think it would be a good idea to have you lead part of this group along the Wyle River."

"Nolan I would love to. It would be an honor."

"Don't get too excited. We'll see how everything else is going first because we've already lost a lot of men."

"What are the plans?"

"We're sending your group, not to fight, but to retrieve the sword. It will not be an easy task."

"Yes, I know, not with Serpentine having it."

"Also, Olof, keep the king in your prayers. I received a note saying that he is bedridden with a terrible cold."

"Is he going to be alright?"

"He's tough and strong, just like his father was. Go ahead and get ready, it's time to move forward."

Nolan walked off to lead the group through the dark, treacherous caves.

* * * * *

"Boy, you really cost us big this time, Olof."

"What do you mean, Greg?"

"You let the Dark Wolves get that sword from you."

145

"Well, I didn't let them, they stole it from us."

"We're doomed now. Thanks a lot, Olof."

As Greg was about to walk away, I grabbed him by the arm. "Hold on, Greg. Let's talk for a minute. I don't know what your problem is with me, but we need to talk about it."

"Get your hands off me!"

I slowly took my hand away from his arm. "Okay, now let's talk about it."

"There's nothing to talk about. I hate you!"

" How can you hate me, Greg? You don't even know me."

"My father told me enough about you."

"Oh really? What did he tell you?"

"That's none of your business!"

"That's no way to talk to your elders, Greg."

"Why should I respect you? You've been in prison all my life!"

146

"But I'm still your uncle!"

"You're not my uncle! Now get out of my sight!"

Greg ran off to get as far away from me as possible.

* * * * *

"I always knew you were going to come home someday, Olof."

"How did you know that, Orion?"

"I just felt it in my heart that my big brother was going to come home one day. Momma knew it too. She used to tell Daddy at dinnertime every night that Olof will be home eating with us one day."

"Well, Momma had some kind of faith because I thought I was going to rot in that dungeon. So tell me Orion, what's it like being married and having children of your own?"

"It's different, but I love every moment of it. My husband is my best friend. We talk all the time about everything."

"Maybe one day I will find a good girl and get married."

"You never know, Olof. Daddy took it real hard when Momma died."

"Did he?"

"Oh yes. He didn't go to work for two months and he wouldn't speak to any of us. But he's a lot better now."

"That's good. It's strange seeing our father as an old man. He moves a lot slower, needs more rest than usual, and it takes him a hour to finish a meal."

Orion almost fell over laughing. I just smiled.

"After the war, Olof, are you going back to the village Pasqual?"

"Probably not. There are too many bad memories there."

"Well, I can understand that."

"Tell me something, Orion. Why doesn't Greg like me?"

"Syphon never had anything good to say about you. He planted a lot of negative seeds in Greg's head."

"How long had that been going on?"

"Ever since our mother died. That's when I really noticed it. Don't worry about it, Olof. In time Greg will come around."

"I can't wait 'til that day comes."

"It's getting pretty cold out at night. You can tell winter is coming. If the snow comes first, we'll never make it over the mountains."

Phlax came over to join us. "Now we're all one happy family again," Phlax said.

Except for Greg, I thought to myself. "So where's Nigel?"

"Over there playing with Greg. Those two are inseparable. They're the best of friends. They were born two days apart from each other," Phlax replied.

"It's going to be a cold winter. It's already pretty cold once the sun goes down," said Orion, tactfully changing the subject.

"I can't wait until this war is over," I said.

"Me too," replied Phlax.

"I'm going to get some sleep. I'll see you two tomorrow," Orion said.

* * * * *

"This day was rougher than most.
We trained all day. I sparred against Nolan
the whole time. He never seemed to get tired
--or maybe I'm just getting old. My skills
are definitely being sharpened. Every bone
in my body aches. The night air must have

gotten the best of my father because he's

sick. It makes me wonder if he's going to

live through this journey.

Olof, the

Great"

I stood by the fire warming myself. It was pretty

late. Everyone was asleep except for my father.

"I hear you're still not feeling well."

"I feel a little better, but I'm still pretty weak. I've

been coughing up blood here and there. It's just old age.

Your bones become brittle and you get sick more. How

have you been, Olof?"

"I've been thinking a lot more lately."

"Thinking about what?"

"Our family, the war, and what's going to become

of us as a people."

"It's good to see us as a family starting all over again."

"Well, yes, that's good. But I think it's not the same."

"What do you expect, Olof? It's been twenty years. Everything can't stay the same. Your siblings grew up and had families of their own. I know it's a difficult adjustment for you because it seems as if time stood still for you."

"Well it did!"

"Trust me, Olof, you've changed too. You probably don't realize it because you're looking at how everyone else has changed."

"Maybe you're right. That's something I need to think about."

* * * * *

"The big day is here, Olof!"

"What do you mean, Nolan?"

"We finally made it to the end of the caves. We've come to the Solo Mountains. Now I have an assignment for you. I want you to take Balsk, Rinu, Vine, Dranu, Cantu, Walas, Vil, Knost, Celon, Karas, Jamgu, Ari, Mosta, Lean, Whilt, Sho, Makka, Tira, Garl, Tiris, Borak, Ryan, and ten thousand soldiers down the Wyle River. You must build a lot of boats. The enemy will not expect anyone to be taking the river. Once you invade the castle, don't waste any time fighting off their troops. There will be too many of them. Just get the Sword of Judah and make it out alive. Those are your orders."

"Yes, sir! But what about my family?"

"They will be in good hands with us. You will make it there right before us, but once we get there the war is will be on. Do you feel ready for this?"

"I'm nervous, but I'll be alright."

I gathered my group, said goodbye to my family, and led my group down to the river to begin building the boats.

* * * * *

The first week was spent chopping trees. I was so worn out I didn't want to see another tree for the rest of my life. We all got very little sleep because we were committed to a schedule. If we slacked up and lost even one day, Nolan and his group would make it to the castle before us and our plan would fail.

We were now building the boats. I wondered how my father was doing. We hadn't received any letters from the others. We could only hope that the other groups were doing as well as we was.

"I'm tired, Olof! We can't keep this up day after day. I have to get more rest," Garl complained.

"We're almost done. You can get plenty of rest when the last few boats are finished," I said.

"We're not your slaves, Olof! This is ridiculous. I say we stop now and get some rest," Mosta said.

"You guys need to quit complaining. We have a task to complete," Balsk said.

Mosta, Whilt, Lean, and Garl stopped working on the boats and went to rest. There was nothing I could say I knew they were exhausted. "Okay, we're all going to stop for the night and get some rest," I said.

There was a sigh of relief from the whole group. I lay down, totally exhausted from the many long days of hard work and immediately fell asleep. That night I had a terrible dream. Both of my legs and arms were tied down, not with ropes, but by vipers. Along came a large red snake and said, "Well, Olof. Why don't you just give up?"

"Never! I'm not quitting!"

"You should. You've already lost the Sword of Judah. Now you're sending this group to their own funerals. You can't win this war."

"Who are you?"

"I'm Serpentine, the destroyer. Quit now before more lives are lost."

"No, we're not going to quit!"

"If you go home now, I'll let you live. But if you come to my castle, I will kill you and everyone with you!"

Then the snake rushed at me with its mouth wide open, ready to devour me. I woke up in a puddle of sweat. I couldn't get back to sleep the rest of the night. Quite honestly, I didn't want to, so I stayed up and prayed. At first light, we were back to diligently working on the boats. Everyone worked a lot faster because they were well rested.

"Olof, how does it feel to be leader?" Makka asked.

"It's different," I said.

"I think you'll do good. My father always said that about you."

Makka was hammering when she suddenly collapsed from weariness. I ran over to help her. "Are you okay?"

"I guess I need more rest," she said.

As I helped Makka to her feet, about a hundred underground warriors burst out of the ground. "It's all over for you, Olof!"

It was Mulcham. He lunged at me, swinging his long sharp claws. I blocked each swing with my sword, but Mulcham used his tail to sweep my legs and I fell to the ground. He tried to jump on top of me, but I kicked him in the face. Mulcham swung very fast and cut my face. I felt the blood running down to my neck. He opened his mouth and a green liquid spewed out and hit me in my eyes. I tried to open my eyes, but the green liquid had blinded me. My eyes burned intensely. I stood up, but tripped over something and fell into the river and was swept downstream. There was nothing I could do. I was able to swim enough to stay afloat.

As I floated along, I heard a lot of noise. It was the ogres. They were coming to finish us off. I stayed underwater for long periods of time, hoping they wouldn't notice me. Thoughts began running through my head about the whole group being killed and me being the lone survivor. All I could do was pray for them. The pain in my eyes was intense and I still couldn't see anything, not even a blur. I hoped I would survive in this river.

* * * * *

"Dear King Grace,

We have split up into two groups. I haven't heard from their leader, Olof, since we split up. We've been fighting against the ogres this whole time. Now we're in the Solo Mountains. Within two weeks we should be at the Varcraine Castle. There

have been many difficult battles and we've

lost almost nine thousand men. Keep us in

your prayers, my king.

Nolan"

The king was in a state of shock from the letter.

"There's no way they're going to survive once they get to

the castle. They've lost too many men," the king spoke

nervously.

"Sire, should we send another group of men?" Narx

asked.

"No. There's no way they could make it in time. I

wonder if the other groups have any survivors."

"Sire, hopefully the other groups are doing better

than Nolan's."

"All we can do now is pray." King Grace heaved a

weary sigh.

* * * * *

I finally got my eyesight back. When I looked down the river, I couldn't believe my eyes. Varcraine Castle was right in front of me. It looked like it was made of charcoal black stone and there were dead trees surrounding it. To my surprise, even the river was black as I got closer to the castle.

Once I made it out of the water, I hid in some bushes. My stomach roared like a lion because I hadn't eaten anything in three days. *I pray that there are some survivors. There's no way I can do this by myself.* As I gazed at the castle from a distance, I could see that ogres heavily guarded it.

I knelt in the bushes, barely moving, to write a letter to Nolan.

"Hello Nolan,

This is Olof. Mulcham defeated our forces. As far as I know, I'm the only survivor. There was nothing to eat in this desolate area. I looked through my backpack hoping to find something. Just my luck, it was empty, so I prayed to God for some food.

* * * * *

The next day when I woke up and opened my eyes, there was an apple in front of me. I devoured, it seeds and all. God had sent me an apple! I hoped that Nolan had received my letter by now. I glanced at the castle. There weren't as many ogres guarding it now. The drawbridge was being lowered and I could see an evil black knight with red eyes leading at least a thousand soldiers out.

Maybe Nolan and his troops are doing okay. Here I am right, near the castle, like a sitting duck waiting to be killed by an archer. If only I had about a thousand troops we could raid this place. That's just wishful thinking because it's only me for right now. As I sat there I opened up the book, *Poems of the Lion* and the verse that jumped

out at me was "Sun of righteousness, arise with healing in

his wings." What a powerful verse -- food for my soul.

I heard a noise. I looked back in the direction it

came from and saw some boats coming down the river.

Some of our troops had survived. I ran from the bushes to

greet them.

"It's so good to see you," I said.

"You, too!" said Garl. "We thought you were dead,

Olof."

"No, I'm still alive. How many soldiers survived?" I

asked.

"We have only a thousand," replied Mosta.

"God answered my prayer. Everyone, get some rest

tonight because we're going to invade the castle tomorrow

morning. Our mission is to get the Sword of Judah and

escape. Nolan's orders were not to fight, only to get the

sword."

"Don't worry, Olof, we'll get it," Jamgu said confidently.

"So what's our plan, Olof?" Makka asked.

"Which of you can climb walls?" I asked.

"I can, Olof," Ryan responded with excitement in his voice.

"Ryan, I need you to climb the wall all the way to the top. I believe the room at the top is where the sword is being kept."

"What if someone sees him?" Karas asked.

"Hopefully, no one will. We're going to divert the ogres by drawing them out to fight us," I said.

"I hope this works because if it doesn't, Ryan is a dead man," said Garl in a doubtful tone.

"Why do you always talk so negative?" Tira asked.

Lean quickly interrupted. "We've been spotted. Ogres are coming our way!"

Tira pulled out her sword and charged at the ogres. The rest of us followed. A gruesome fight took place. I shot my crossbow and cut the rope connected to the drawbridge. The bridge came down on top of ten of the ogres. We ran inside the castle as quickly as we could. Ryan ran ahead trying to find the stairs that led to the room at the top of the castle. A headless warrior riding a horse came after me, swinging a mace. He aimed it at me, but I moved out of the way. It hit the ground with a thud, the spiked ball leaving a crater in the earth. Tira shot one of the ogres in the eye with her crossbow and he disappeared.

"That's their weakness, men. Aim at their eye!" I yelled.

Tira found the stairway. "Come on, Ryan. It's your chance to be a hero."

The sky suddenly turned completely black. I looked and immediately realized there were large ravens overhead led by Vulcore.

"Get them," she screamed to the ravens. "Take no prisoners! We want them dead, all of them!" Vulcore swooped down and grabbed the crossbow from Tira's hand. Tira ran at her, swinging her sword, but missed her as the bird woman flipped and landed behind her. Vulcore kicked Tira, her claws causing deep cuts in Tira's flesh.

"You are no match for me," Vulcore said in an arrogant tone.

Tira went to swing again, but Vulcore flipped and landed on top of Tira's shoulders. The bird woman dug her claws into Tira's skin, then picked her up and flew as high as she could, then released her. Tira fell to her death. Garl's heart broke as he watched the whole scene, helpless to save her.

Ryan ran up the stairs. He was tired, sweaty, and his legs were hurting. The higher he climbed, the darker it became. He could barely see in front of him. Ryan had his sword ready in case any Dark Wolves popped out. When he heard any noise, he immediately started tiptoeing. Fear gripped his heart as he approached the last few stairs, which led to topmost room.

Ryan peeked into the room, looked around, but saw no one. He spotted the Sword of Judah. There it was, right in front of him and Serpentine was nowhere to be seen. Ryan ran over, grabbed the sword, and then turned to dash down the stairs that would lead him to freedom. Before he took his first step, the door slammed shut. He pulled on it with all his might, but he was unable to get it open. Finally, out of frustration, he tried to kick it open, to no avail.

A two-headed man appeared. One of his heads was that of a deformed man, while the other was a serpent. Ryan felt fear as he saw pure evil, face-to-face for the first time.

"Put the sword down, Ryan," said the creature in a calm voice.

"No!" Ryan responded, trembling.

Ryan ran to the balcony, his eyes searching the many combatants in the field of battle far below. In a matter of seconds, he spotted Olof.

"Olof, Olof, Olof!" Ryan yelled as loud as he could.

I looked up when I realized someone was calling my name. Ryan threw the Sword of Judah from the balcony. It landed in the earth right in front of me.

Ryan turned around and looked at Serpentine. "Do what you will, old serpent. My purpose is fulfilled!"

A snake appeared in Serpentine's hand. He threw it like a spear into Ryan's heart. Ryan had a smile on his face as he collapsed to the floor, dead.

I grabbed the sword and yelled, "Retreat men! We have the sword! We have the sword!"

* * * * *

We all ran from the castle and hid in the nearby woods. That short battle cost us almost three hundred troops. No one took it as hard as Garl, who lost his wife Tira. I went over to comfort him.

"It's going to be alright, Garl."

"Olof, save your breath! You've never lost a wife!"

"I know, but I lost a brother and that still hurts every time I think about it."

"I just need some time alone to think." Garl walked off to another part of the forest. Only God knew the pain Garl was experiencing.

I hope the other groups get here soon.

* * * * *

"Your Highness,

All is going well at this time. We've defeated a lot of the enemy forces. As I write this letter, we are getting closer to the castle. We still have about thirty-five thousand troops that are well trained and always ready for battle. We shall see you soon, my king.

Your loyal servant,

War"

King Grace finished reading the letter, and then laid it on the table in front of him. "Well, Narx, it's good to know War and his group are doing well."

"That's true, my king. The closer they get to the castle, the closer we are to victory."

"I've been thinking, Narx."

"About what, my king?"

"About going into hiding. I believe the Dark Wolves' next step might be to invade the castle."

"I think that would be a hasty move, my king."

"But what if I'm right, Narx? What if they do a surprise attack against the castle?"

"They wouldn't dare try that, my king. It would be a very foolish move."

"Maybe you're right, Narx. Fear is just getting the best of me, I guess."

* * * * *

We resumed extensive training every day for the next month as we waited patiently for the other troops to arrive. We hadn't heard anything from Nolan yet. Maybe he never received my letter or perhaps he had a lot of things on his mind. Makka became an expert shot with the crossbow. She lacked the strength to mastering sword fighting, but she knew how to use a dagger. As I sat by the tree watching them, God appeared to me in a vision.

The lion from my dreams walked towards me. "You're doing great, Olof. Let me explain something to you. Only the Sword of Judah or the chosen ones can kill Serpentine and his generals. They can be defeated no other way. Guard that sword with your life if you want to win the war."

"Yes, God, I'll guard the sword with my life."

"Help is coming, Olof. Your friends will be here soon. You're making me proud. You've become the leader I called you to be. I must be going now. Remember, I'm with you always."

"Thanks, God."

* * * * *

"What are you doing up so early, Olof?" Balsk asked.

"I was just talking to God," I said.

"That's a good thing to be doing. God answers our prayers in many ways when we least expect it."

"So how long have you been a Christian, Balsk?"

"Thirty years, Olof."

"Wow! How have those thirty years been?"

"They've been the best years of my life. God has taught me so much. What about you, Olof?"

"It has only been a few months."

"It may seem like a short time, but God has really used you to make impact in a lot of lives."

"Do you think so, Balsk?"

"Oh, I know so, Olof. You have touched this whole group, your family and all the others. Olof, sometimes you never know the impact you've made on someone else until years later. While serving God these thirty years I watched my whole family come to God one by one-- my wife, my five sons, and my daughter Makka. I never thought that I would live to see that day but I did. Makka amazes me most as I watch her prayer life develop. She always reads the *Poems of the Lion*. Now that's impressive."

"That's awesome. I can't wait to see my father and my brother come to Christ."

"It all happens in time, Olof. We want everything to happen immediately, but it doesn't always do that."

"What made you turn your life over to God?"

"Well, Olof. I felt as if my life was going nowhere. My life was being destroyed by sin and I needed a way out, so I turned to God."

"Wow! And now it's thirty years later."

"Yes, thirty years. How time flies!"

* * * * *

"How did they invade the Varcraine Castle and take back the sword? Tell me, how did this happen?" Serpentine demanded to know.

"Master, I don't know how it happened," Golan replied fearfully.

"That wasn't what I wanted to hear. Now they have the sword and we still haven't eliminated one of the tribes. Golan, I blame you. If you had a head, I would certainly cut it off! Now tell me about the ten groups the king sent."

"They have lost a lot of soldiers, but they are still on their way. Not one group has been completely wiped out," Waldor reported.

"This is the plan. Don't fight their forces anymore until they get to the castle, then we can crush them completely. We shall once and for all destroy the Fighting Eagles. After we crush them, then we shall attack the royal castle in full force and take care of King Grace and any other heirs to the throne. We must stop the chosen ones from being born. The prophecy must be stopped. Also, whoever brings me the Sword of Judah shall receive ten thousand gold coins and I shall give them more power as well."

* * * * *

"Greg, come on, we have to practice our sword fighting," Nigel urged.

"I don't feel like it. Why do we have to do this every day? It doesn't matter, we're going to die anyway," Greg replied.

"How do you know, Greg?"

"Nigel, look at what's happened so far. Our army always loses to the Dark Wolves, every time."

"But God promises us victory in the *Poems of the Lion.*"

"So what does it say?"

"It says that there will come a time when evil will be defeated in the end."

"When will that be, Nigel?"

"Once the twelve chosen ones come forth."

"They always talk about those chosen ones, but they've never come."

"You must have faith, Greg."

"Well, I don't. It never helped my mother. God didn't rescue her when the invading army came into our village and killed her."

"Greg, God is there for you, but you have to believe."

"Well, I don't believe in God, Nigel. He hasn't done anything for me!"

"That's what you think. He's already done a lot for you."

"Nigel, save it for someone who wants to listen to it. Let's just get our swords and go practice. It doesn't matter, we'll be dead as soon as Serpentine catches us."

* * * * *

"God, I need you to protect Olof and his group. Lord, I pray that you will guide him. Oh, that you could encourage and strengthen him as a leader. Help him to make wise choices. When he's feeling lonely, comfort him,

Lord. Let him know that you're with him every step of the way. Deliver him from doubt and disbelief. Don't let him grow weary of doing the right thing. I pray that the rest of the troops will support his decisions as well."

Tiris got up off of his knees after he ended his prayers.

Nolan walked over to him. "I liked those prayers, Tiris. I hope you put in a few for me."

"Of course I did. I prayed for all of us."

"If everyone was like you, the world would be a better place."

"Thanks, Nolan. How far do you think we are from the castle?"

"Not too far, we're almost there. We should be meeting the others soon."

"Do you think our troops are ready?"

"Honestly, I hope they are. When the battle takes place, we'll find out."

"We should be in good shape, Nolan. There are plenty of good men left."

"Well, let's get going. We have a long journey ahead of us."

* * * * *

"Olof, the cavalry has arrived!"

"What do you mean, Dranu?"

"All of the groups are here. While you were asleep, Nolan sent a messenger over. It's time to fight."

"Then wake everyone up. We'll go meet Nolan and await his orders."

Dranu went to wake everyone to meet with Nolan and the others. I was so grateful to see Tiris, my father, Phlax, Orion, and their children. I hugged each one as tears of joy filled my eyes. I never thought this day would ever come. Nolan rose to speak.

"We're all doing well and the time for war is upon us. Now we must strike the enemy. When we invade the castle that will be the sign for the other groups to attack. Our plan is to take down Serpentine. We must get to his room and kill him. Once Serpentine and his generals are dead, their whole army will die, too. That's the prophecy. Let's go, Fighting Eagles!"

We mounted our horses and moved forward with anticipation. The ogres were the first forces we came in contact with. Phlax dove off his horse, tackled an ogre, and began beating him fiercely. Makka shot ogre after ogre with her crossbow. All their target practice was definitely paying off. The other groups came down the various trails ready to fight. I watched as some of the ogres yanked men off of their horses and beat them with clubs. Swalo swung his staff like a sword. Every ogre that he hit disappeared. For the first time, our army was winning.

The black knight with red eyes came with some soldiers ready to fight. Lexon was viciously sending our men to early graves one by one. Once I made eye contact with him, he came after me. We clashed swords and I knocked him off his horse. He hit me in the face with his shield, knocking me to the ground. I held on to the Sword of Judah with all my might, remembering what God told me. When I got up off the ground, Lexon grabbed me and threw me as far as he could. Tiris came over to help me, but he was no match for Lexon. I ran over to help him, but was knocked to the ground again. A hundred wolves came charging at our men. Lexon pulled an arrow from his quiver and shot Phlax in the back. Phlax cried out in pain.

"You'd better go help your brother, Olof!" said Lexon.

I ran over to Phlax and dragged him away from the battle.

"Thanks, Olof. I needed that," Phlax said.

"Save your breath, you've been injured pretty bad."

Makka ran over to Phlax and me. "Get back out there, Olof. I'll help your brother. Go! You're our only hope."

I ran back ready to meet Lexon. Tiris was nowhere in sight. *Maybe Tiris is dead*, I wondered. The battle raged on as I saw our forces penetrating the castle. Serpentine's days were numbered. Vulcore swooped low, knocking me to the ground. Garl saw her and chased her with his sword.

"So, you are going to get revenge?"

"Yes I am," said Garl. "It's life for life!"

Vulcore kicked him in the head. He quickly recovered and swung his sword. She avoided it, grabbed him by the neck, and threw him down to the ground. Garl grabbed her by the hair, threw her down and punched her in the face seven times. Vulcore flew off in a panic, knowing she was defeated. The large ravens swooped down, attacking our men. Mulcham popped up out of the ground and grabbed me from behind. I couldn't break away from his grip. Nolan came up and stabbed him in the back. He scurried underground with a sword lodged in his back. Orion was fighting Waldor. I couldn't believe it, my little sister had become a warrior. The battlefield extended from the Varcraine Castle all the way to the nearby mountains. Suddenly, I was once again fighting Lexon, a formidable opponent who wasted no time trying to gain the advantage. He knocked me to the ground and tried to gut me like a fish, but again, I was able to get out of the way in time.

He turned and looked at Makka. "The chosen seed is in her!" Lexon swung his sword, cutting her stomach open. Makka slumped over a large rock gasping for air. "NOOO!!" I screamed as I ran toward Lexon, knocking him off a cliff. I felt a stinging pain in my chest and I realized he had cut me with his sword when we made contact. Blood poured from my chest and I grew weaker and weaker. I fell on my knees, gripping the Sword of Judah tightly against my chest. My father rushed to my aid.

"Olof, you can't die on me, you can't!"

"I feel weak. I don't think I'm going to make it."

"You must, Olof. You can't die!"

"I'm going home, Father. I'm going home to God. "

Pereal began sobbing uncontrollably and embraced me.

"Father, you need to serve God. He loves you."

As I closed my eyes I saw God, the great lion. "Well done, Olof, my good and faithful servant."

I watched as my soul left my body bound for Heaven, while the battle continued. Although the Fighting Eagles tried their best, they were unable to prevail. The Dark Wolves were on a rampage, slaughtering everyone in sight. The army of Fighting Eagles was completely crushed.

Serpentine came out of the castle and yelled to his troops. "Search all the bodies. Find the Sword of Judah. Ha! Ha! We've won the war!"

His ogres searched all the bodies on the ground. They lifted up the body of a woman and noticed a wing sticking out of the cut on her stomach, but it meant nothing to them, so they dropped her. After they had searched the entire battlefield, Tarlenum came back to report to Serpentine.

"What do you mean the Sword of Judah is gone?"

* * * * *`